FANNIE

Rebecca F. John's first novel, *The Haunting of Henry Twist* (Serpent's Tail, 2017), was shortlisted for the Costa First Novel Award. Her story 'The Glove Maker's Numbers' was shortlisted for the Sunday Times EFG Short Story Award 2015. She won the PEN International New Voices Award 2015, and was the British participant of the 2016 Scritture Giovani project. In 2017, she was on the Hay Festival's 'The Hay 30' list. Her stories have been broadcast on Radio 4 and published in *Clown Shoes* (Parthian, 2015). She is launching her own press, Aderyn, in January and her children's fantasy novel will be published by Firefly Press in 2022. She lives in Swansea with her dogs, where she writes, reads, and walks to excess.

To all the women who have been silenced

First published in Great Britain in 2022 by Honno Press
'Ailsa Craig', Heol y Cawl, Dinas Powys, Vale of Glamorgan,
Wales, CF64 4AH

1 2 3 4 5 6 7 8 9 10

A catalogue record for this book is available from the British Library.

Published with the financial support of the Books Council of Wales.

ISBN: 9781912905515 (paperback)
ISBN: 9781912905522 (ebook)

Cover design and chapter heading illustrations by Kari Brownlie

Text design: Elaine Sharples
Printed and bound by CPI Group (UK) Ltd, Croydon, CR0 4YY

FANNIE

Rebecca F. John

Prologue

Fannie lies on her side, a smile shadowing her lips, and watches the embroidered portière swell and drop. The fabric is a light cotton, weighted slightly by the stitched stems and rosebuds which vein its surface, but not heavy enough to resist the wind which paws at it through the open window. On the sill, a wren trills. The morning is already warm with the breath of passing factory workers and the scent of baking bread, and, beyond the wren's song, there comes the distant drone of chatter. Fannie leans into her lover, and is surprised not to find him clammy under her nose. They have slept with the night on their skin, and his jaw, his neck, his bare left shoulder, are chilled to stone. Fannie finds a freckle, raised a little against his smooth surface, and touches her tongue tip to it: cold. She wishes, fleetingly, that he truly was the statue he appears when he sleeps. That way, she would never again need to be parted from him. But the wish is chased by a vision, of a creature older and lesser than herself kneeling before his perfect form, begging him to breathe, to breathe, desperate for the simple rise and fall of his chest. She concentrates on his arrhythmic, snort-and-huff snoring, soothes her thoughts with

1

his jagged inhalations. Hidden behind the portière, the shabby room Fannie rents – visited by pattering mice and creeping damp – is forgotten. And with it, the rest of the unquiet city. There is only the silvered seven o'clock light, splaying through the window to guillotine the dust. And the moisture her gentleman has left between her legs and under her armpits. And the heat in the rumples of her sheets. There is only the masted galleon of her bed and the places they travel together on it, night after night. And the portière – a billowing sail, blinding her to everything which lies ahead.

Abandonment

The walk to and from the factory takes her twice daily by the docks: firstly, in the flat, murky pre-dawn, when she dashes towards her half-past-six start, her head low and her ears straining past the groan of incoming ships and their thrown ropes for any sign of danger; and latterly in the approaching clutch of night, when the ladies who holler and moan from the city's darkest corners sneak around the boatyards and along the jetties to begin shifts of their own.

This morning, the air is cold and Fannie pulls her long coat tightly around her. It is threadbare and mended with two different styles of button: one brass, the other silver. It embarrasses her, but it is the only one she owns, and she has no means of replacing it. She hopes at least to become invisible inside it. In this city, she has learnt, staying unseen is the most reliable way of keeping from trouble.

Winter mists draw the day's first cargo ships in from the salt-black sea like beckoning hands and Fannie pauses for a moment to watch two vessels drift into view, silvered hulls, then masts, then sails seeming to settle into existence before her eyes. A pair of ghost ships made tangible. The briny stink of shallow tides, just swallowing the mudflats where, come midday, city children will trudge out and lark for treasures. She rests her elbows on the stone balustrade of the narrow bridge, where sometimes her curiosity tempts her to stop, and exhales.

Her breath rises before her in two smoky pillars. Another pair: to match the ships, and their sails, and the two gulls squabbling over a shed feather some steps away. Everywhere she looks, she is confronted by pairs. It causes envy to swell in Fannie. She, too, constitutes one half of an unbreakable pair — at least, so long as the foreman doesn't find out — but it is not the coupling she had imagined. She had thought they would be three, not two.

One of the ships thuds against the wooden jetty and the sound sets off a scurrying. From every darkened doorway, from the shadows of the ships' skeletons, from between the sand-held stilts at the dry end of the jetty, the rats come: claws scritching, tails ribboning, fur glistening. They are followed almost immediately by the women. The women have painted over their sicknesses with powder and rouge. They have fastened feathers of mauve and fuchsia and indigo over the thinning patches on their scalps. They have hoisted up their skirts and pulled down their lace-topped camisoles. They are clowns with plumped breasts and poised legs. Their perfume plumes around them, and Fannie turns her head slightly from the cloying, flowery scent which catches on the wind and, stealing between her lips, stings her throat. But still she

4

watches them, parading down the jetty like a chorus of showgirls.

'Oi, oi, sailors!' one bellows. Her voice is vulgar and harsh in the early quiet. It matches the heavy clunk of her boots over the wooden slats. She walks with her legs set at a hospitable distance, as though she herself has been to sea and not regained her balance. 'Come on, chaps. We've been waiting on you. Nice to have a friendly welcome, isn't it, ay?'

On the decks of the ships, the blackened shapes of men, made larger by thick, belted coats and stiff hats, cluster at the bulwarks, haloed by their steaming breath. Leaning over the railings, they whoop and holler as though they are at a racetrack, tickets held in their clenched fists and certain of a winner. To Fannie, they might just as well be leering down at a pack of animals, for all the kindness they will show. She knows too well what cruelty men are capable of.

She watches the women wave their handkerchiefs and tussle with each other for the best position along the jetty, laughing too loudly as they shove and thrust in a manner which persuades their breasts to tremble. *Can I interest you in my jellied fruits, sir?* Fannie permits herself a gentle smile. Pickled whelks, more like. There is no sweetness to be found under those bodices. And good enough! She thinks it doubtful any of their customers would deserve the taste of sugar.

As the men begin to disembark, she turns and continues her walk. Overhead, the moon is the curve of a swan's neck, waning into invisibility. Leaving the water at her back, Fannie steps towards the rows of merchants' buildings she must pass between and, quite by accident, begins trailing a plush blue-grey cat as it struts through slants of shade. She watches it slink and dart, at ease in this imposing place. Set into the columns of the grandest establishments, the moulded heads of lions and horses stare down at passers-by, rendering the buildings as magnificent as the ships and galleons which finance them. They are mostly dark at this hour, save for the occasional lit window behind which some young apprentice labours over his figures. Today, Fannie counts three. She feels a swell of affection for them, these industrious young men she imagines. She, too, prefers to begin the day before the rest of the city. She, too, thrives on the quiet stillness of possibility. She hopes that when each new day dawns, it will be less lonely than the one before. That is all the ambition she holds for herself now. Her every other thought is for another.

The buildings grow smaller as she travels further from the docks. Two streets on, she is stealing past the three-storey townhouses of wealthy families, trying to hold herself so delicately that she moves in silence. Always, she imitates the ballerinas she saw, and was instantly captivated by, on her sole visit to the theatre. When she rose from the dense velvet of her seat, she concentrated on the direction of her every muscle and sinew: first she stretched out her back and found that she had been neglecting perhaps two inches of height; then, after pulling on her coat, she focused on furling her fingers back into a pleasingly dainty position. It was her way of taking control of the body which was beginning to feel so strange to her that dark winter, with its new poking hairs and the bulging

flesh she could not seem to strap flat beneath her clothes. She
has held to it since. And perhaps it makes a flat, papery
creature of her, to stand so straight, to move so carefully, but
it is the only way Fannie knows to face the world.

On the doorsteps of each greyed house, the morning
newspapers wait, curled neatly inside tied string. Behind their
gleaming windowpanes, candlelight gutters as servants lay fires
and nursemaids scoop babies from their white, cotton sheets.

One wooden pane has been slid up a little and, through the
opened wedge, an infant's cry blares. Fannie stops, to quiet the
even click-click of her boots and to breathe away the sudden
clench at her stomach. Still, she responds to that wail for the
breast. Even after all this time.

The cat, recognising its home, makes an abrupt right turn,
flows up the front steps, and disappears. Fannie straightens up
and continues.

Less than ten minutes later, she arrives at the factory. The
doors are black and hulking and perhaps fifteen feet high.
Fannie pauses under a burning lamp, searching for some
excuse to delay taking the last breath of clean air she will enjoy
for twelve hours. Her hair has dampened in the mists, and the
waves which hang below her bonnet are straggly and dull. She
catches a limp ringlet between her fingers and marvels again
at how exactly its golden shade had matched her love's. How
surprised she'd been – having supposed they would create a
child exactly in their like – to find their new-born daughter's
hair that tone darker. As she climbs the factory steps, Fannie
slips off her coat. The formerly royal-blue material has paled

unevenly, and she does not want the other women to see its map-like patches. She folds it over her arm, inside out, and, moving purposefully, fails to notice a neat letter slip from her torn interior pocket and glide to the ground.

Her hand is on the door handle when a call issues from behind her.

'Miss.' A man's voice.

She spins around to find one of the delivery men crouched in the gloom the factory casts over the pavements.

'Yours?' he asks, proffering an envelope which is pinched between his forefinger and thumb.

Fannie trips back down the steps and, snatching up the envelope, clutches it to her chest. She is suddenly breathless.

The man rises slowly. The smile he had been wearing falls away. He is at least two years younger than Fannie: perhaps nineteen. His light-brown moustache hairs are sparser than those concentrated around his chin. In bending to retrieve her letter, he has wetted one leg of his trousers at the knee. He brushes at it absently.

'Thank you,' Fannie manages to say, showing the man a quick smile. 'I'm sorry. That's kind of you. I just...'

'It's an important letter,' the man finishes, relaxing again and finally assuming his full height.

'Yes.' Fannie nods. 'It's an important letter.'

The man extends his hand a second time – for an introductory shake – and opens his mouth, ready to share his name. Fannie does not want to hear it. She does not want to exchange pleasantries with any man. Since her abandonment, she has remained entirely chaste. The factory girls tease her about it, her landlady questions the fact with crossed arms and a raised eyebrow, but Fannie will not be swayed. She has a different purpose now from the one she envisaged before she met her gentleman, when the city was her own whirring carousel, and she has dedicated every ounce of herself to it. She is glad to. It is for love that she works six twelve-hour days a week in the factory, sewing garments for women whose circumstances have fallen more favourably than her own. For love that she eats only a meagre supper before tucking her wages into her pillowcase and, at the end of each week, posting them to the innkeepers she must pay. For love that she rushes to curl into her bedsheets each night and – the portière always drawn back now, for she does not wish to remember how it felt to vanish behind it – dream her way into the shining countryside, where her daughter plays in the fields, and sings, and waits for her.

Needlework

The workroom has always put Fannie in mind of a galley ship. Eight narrow wooden tables run along its considerable length. To one side of each, there is a straight wooden bench, on which the girls might be fortunate to sit undisturbed for an hour before the foreman skulks behind them and questions whether they are working hard enough. The tables are set four feet apart – distant enough so that the girls are not tempted to speak to the rows in front or behind them, but close enough so that the foreman, strutting between them like a full-bellied fox, can reach out his filthy, black-nailed hands to the girls on his left or his right with equal facility. Though the fires are lit on those days when a visit from the mayor is expected, more often the foreman insists that they work with only their lamps to warm them. Through the winter, the girls remain in their coats and bonnets all day and the factory walls run with damp. Drips of condensation drop from the ceiling beams and extinguish the flames of their candles. The girls make fists and try to breathe the feeling back into their red and swollen knuckles. The mayor, who owns the factory, is well-intentioned – they all agree on that, in whispers – but he is too busy to notice that the foreman takes pleasure in their discomfort. The promise of its easing is a commodity he attempts to trade – 'for the right price,' he suggests, leering. The gaps between his teeth are grouted with yellowed tobacco residue; his words are met with winces. Fannie does not know how many of the girls have submitted to his advances, but judging by the angry glances which pass between the foreman and the jet-haired supervisor, she suspects that at least one has, and that the outcome was at best disappointing.

As she unfolds the first garment she will work on and flattens it over the table, Fannie plans the sentences she will dictate to the letter-writer later that evening, ready to be sent into the countryside, to the couple she has trusted with her whole heart.

I can pay. Anything, so that you might purchase the medicine she needs. I just need a little time. A week, if you please. Within a week, I will find the money. I beg you: do not stop administering the medicine…

She longs to dash to the letter-writer now and spill out her reply, but she has no money to pay him with until the shift's end. Besides, she cannot risk her position at the factory. Every morning and every night, she sees what becomes of the women who could not find work as a seamstress or a lady's maid or a tavern girl. Fannie sews even as her fingers bleed to ensure that she keeps up with the more experienced girls. She cannot afford to be left behind.

Today, she is first to arrive. She braces herself against the cold, licks the end of her cotton, and threads her needle with a deftness on which she no longer needs to concentrate. Against the quiet, there is only the gentle rasp of cotton through cotton and the in and out of her breathing. The two fall automatically into time. In; pierce. Out; draw through. In...

Despite herself, Fannie remembers the roll and hush of the tide, the day she and her gentleman took a train to the seaside. They'd giggled and simpered all the way: at each other's childlike excitement; at the twitching of the man in the opposite seat's moustache as he sat back, arms crossed over his ample belly, and slumbered; at the jouncing and rattling of the train along the tracks.

The sand, when they finally stepped onto it, was ragged shingle: curls of pale baby's ear and shards of broken angel wings, the protruding points of hidden red conches and the shining grey fingers of razor clams, the black-and-cream rounded gleam of jingle shells and the ridged blue fans of bay scallops, the sickles of half-buried lightning whelks. They tiptoed over them, stopping to pluck them up, lay them on their palms, and study their swirls and bumps and crevices. Fannie's gentleman knew many of their names. He told them to her, accompanied by the screeching of the gulls as they wheeled overhead, and the rush and quiet of the indecisive sea, and the far-off children squealing through a game of chase. And his voice was louder than all that, more immediate than the briny stink of the shallow rock pools they skirted around. His touch more powerful than the weight of all those incoming waves.

Even now, the recollection sends a shudder from the roots of Fannie's hair, along her neck, down her spine, and causes her legs to weaken. That damned man, who so bewitched her that she had waited on his return through two summers, three, dreaming of the autumn they would spend together, and the explanations he would murmur as the leaves blushed and crisped and fell. Their daughter was walking, talking, singing, dancing, worrying over her mother, before Fannie was able to admit, finally, that he was never coming back. That she would grey into old age alone. That he would never know the pleasure of their daughter's chirruping song, or the clutch of her fine pianist's hand, or the sight of her left cheek dimpling when she laughed. There was a secondary grief in that. Lesser than the first, undeniably, but palpable all the same.

The loss of the man felt to Fannie like a shrinking. Or a shrivelling. She fancied all the joy and water and hope and blood being sucked from her, so that, whilst she was alive enough to know the depths of her pain, she was simultaneously mummifying. Soon, her landlady would enter her room and find beneath her bedsheets a dried and shrunken creature, something like those wrinkled, brown oddities men display in cabinets and claim as mermaids – perhaps, in fact, that is what they are. Her gentleman, after all, had not opened up a vast new world she might explore, but only made her smaller within the one she already inhabited. And she hated him for it. And she hated herself more intensely, for having allowed him to do it.

That time, she stayed in her bed for two days and nights, nursing herself through her hideous transformation. When, on the third morning, a slight figure clambered onto her tear-flattened pillow, pressed herself to her back, and traced a half-wilted pink delphinium along her jaw, Fannie stirred herself from her blackest bout of melancholy yet and rose to meet her daughter.

The daughter, she understood then, who must no longer be passed between the neighbouring tenants and half cared for while Fannie went out to work. The daughter who must not be made to rattle around this grimy city just so that her mama could keep her close. Fannie thought then of the inn she had passed by on a trip to the countryside with her gentleman, the two little ones racing around in the yard amongst the scattering chickens, the sunshine lighting their hair and smiles, and knew what she would do. She would give her child a chance at something better. She would offer her an entirely different life.

The prospect of the girl falling ill had never crossed her mind.

The supervisor arrives at the factory to find Fannie unfolding her second garment. She watches from the doorway for a moment as Fannie, head bent as elegantly as a poised carriage horse, smooths the indigo fabric flat, considers her collection of threads, chooses one. Sitting alone in the empty workroom, Fannie is both small and gloriously bright: her hair is a golden glow; her face belongs to a porcelain doll. The supervisor despises her all the more on account of that splinter of her soul which cannot help but admire the younger woman's dedication, her grace, her unbreakable composure.

She has not noticed the red-raw dent at her fingertips, the painful splits in the skin around her fingernails.

'Getting a head start, Fannie?' she says. The girl has been arriving earlier and earlier – pilfering the sleekest runs of fabric, no doubt. The supervisor's words echo in the cavernous room. Fannie does not flinch, as many a disturbed person might. She would not permit herself such weakness, and the supervisor knows it.

'Yes,' Fannie nods. Her voice never alters; always her responses are delivered in the same soft alto. But this morning, she is exhausted – she had not slept a blink last night for worrying about the increasing cost of her daughter's medicine – and the supervisor's words cause her jaw to clench.

'I don't imagine the mayor will visit today,' the supervisor continues, her tone clipped, her feet deliberately heavy over the floorboards. Fannie feels the repeated thud low in her empty stomach. 'There'll be no one to impress.'

'All the same, I might aim to impress myself.' Fannie is not being glib. The answer is truthful. In everything now, she aims for fineness. But ordinarily, she wouldn't voice the thought. At the factory, she has learnt to be quiet, tolerant, unresponsive. 'There is nobility to be found in any job done well, don't you agree?'

Fannie lifts her head to meet the supervisor's eyes and finds them narrowed into blackness. Were she not so hateful, Fannie might tell her that her irises are the most unusual shade of caramel brown, and that her black hair gleams, and that if she should choose to frown a good deal less, she might be quite

16

beautiful. Fannie bows her head again. She does not want to continue this conversation. It will only prove petty and circuitous, as conversations inside the factory walls ever do.

'Any job?' The supervisor's cheeks grow gaunt. 'Even the one them ladies of the night do?'

Fannie uses the last scraps of her energy to summon a smile. The supervisor expects her to retrace her words now, to stumble. But Fannie will not falter at being goaded today.

'Oh, yes,' she replies. 'Even those ladies. After all, they must develop their expertise, mustn't they? And practise. To pretend at pleasure hour after hour, well, I'd imagine it must be exhausting.'

Fannie can hardly believe what she has uttered. The words do not sound like her own, and she knows nothing of those unfortunate ladies but what she glimpses on her walks, but she suspects that the supervisor will think the sentiment unseemly and so could not resist voicing it. The supervisor has extolled the virtues of *making one's way respectably and morally* in a far louder voice since she and the foreman ceased exchanging pleasant words. And indeed, she seems to wane at Fannie's reply. Throwing off her coat, she flusters across to the line of hooks, and fidgets there until the factory doors creak open again and five or six bonneted figures titter inside.

By mid-afternoon, the girls are sniggering into their garments at the frequency with which Fannie checks the clock, their hatred stirred up by the rankled supervisor.

'You haven't got a fellow waiting, have you, Fannie?' croons the worker to her immediate right. 'Finally?'

'Tick-tock, tick-tock,' says another. 'She'll need to persuade *someone* into her bed before she finds herself in the knacker's yard. You're not getting any younger, Fannie.'

'She'll be as wrinkled as her skirts before very long.'

They laugh as one, effecting the cackles of stage witches. The supervisor has long encouraged them in their teasing, but today it contains more venom. Fannie merely raises her chin against it. She is aware, naturally, that this only increases their spiteful urges, but her other option is to lower her head, and that she will not countenance.

'Have you seen, too, how she keeps checking her pocket?'

At this, Fannie betrays her own promise and meets the glinting eye of the girl who has spoken. She is small-chinned and vapid. Her thin nose bears a hump at its bridge, as if broken and never properly healed. 'Ooh, I think I've hit a nerve!' the girl squeals, bumping the shoulder of the supervisor, who she sits close beside.

Fannie feels her ears burning and inwardly curses her fair complexion.

'I have, too,' the girl continues.

'She was fussing with a letter this morning,' joins in a broader girl, with smiling cheeks and a powerful bust.

'Let us see what it says, then, Fannie,' someone crows, making a grab for her pocket.

They are all gabbling at once now, discarding their garments and needles to close around Fannie. She quickly loses track of who is speaking, but she does not blanch as they form a tight circle and begin, like a cluck of chickens, to peck. They

18

have never gone this far before. She should have stayed silent instead of sniping back at the supervisor. But Fannie is tired of silence. Tired of clamping her lips tight around the retorts she ought always to have shot at these women. Tired of endless days and sleepless nights. Tired of longing for the moment when she can return to the inn with a pocketful of coins and open her arms to her shining daughter. She sits erect, her hand clamped over her pocket. Soon, fingers are pinching at the skin of her arms, tearing at the neck of her blouse, pulling the pins from her hair. Strands of hair rip free; her blouse discharges a button. She feels as though flaming match heads are being stubbed out on her scalp, her shoulders, her arms.

When her hand is finally prised loose and her letter stolen, she leaps up and hurls herself at the girl who has taken it, hissing and scratching for all her worth. She does not look up until she has her hands clamped at the thief's collarbone. She sees then that it is the supervisor who holds her letter. For a moment, they all freeze.

'Please,' Fannie gasps. 'It's nothing. It's private.'

The supervisor smirks, then kicks Fannie square in the stomach. 'We'll see, shall we?' she crows, as Fannie stumbles backwards and her arms are grasped by two other girls, who hold her still while the supervisor turns, places one sturdy boot on the bench, and steps up onto the table. Dusty winter light endeavours through the high windows and descends at a frail diagonal. Caught in its blurred shaft, the supervisor is a looming shadow.

Fannie, breathing through the pain at her middle, looks

past her into the rafters, blackened by countless old fires and pocked by the weight of moisture gathering in the smut and grime. They are hung with cobwebs. In one corner, a pair of common house martins nest: flits of blue, brown, and white feather; echoing, spectral chirps.

The supervisor makes a show of clearing her throat.

'Dear Fannie,' she reads. The other girls stand captivated, heads tilted back, lips slightly parted. The two who hold Fannie still grip her tighter. 'I'm sorry to say that the money you send just isn't enough. If you cannot find more, our arrangement will have to be brought immediately to an end. Caring folk, we are, but charity we are not. We have our own to feed.'

The supervisor breaks off, peers over the top of the letter at Fannie.

'And what's this then?' she asks.

Fear thrums through Fannie like a fever. Sweat orbs above her upper lip, rolls between her breasts.

'You're not paying for someone to be cared for, are you, Fannie? You're not … hiding a child, perhaps, are you?'

The deliberation with which she delivers the words persuades Fannie that the supervisor knew everything before she ever had sight of the letter. That lad on the steps earlier – was he in league with her? Fannie slumps onto her knees. What does it matter now? The supervisor will tell the foreman, and the foreman will have his excuse to throw another woman on the mercy of the streets, and she has no idea how she will buy her daughter's medicine without this job.

'I...' she begins, but there are no words to fit her fear. It mutes her.

'Oh, Fannie. Your tongue wasn't so slow this morning. Come, we're all waiting to hear your great secret.'

The supervisor steps back down onto the bench and thence onto the floor. She lowers her face towards Fannie's until Fannie can feel the heat of her nose-tip against her own. She continues in a stage whisper, 'Is there a child, Fannie? Because you know the rules, I'm sure, about unmarried mothers in this factory, don't you? There have always been strict rules here, about unmarried mothers.'

Fannie wants to close her mouth, so that she might shut out the taste of the supervisor's stale threats, but she is panting too heavily. Her chest heaves. The supervisor's eyes are round with feigned innocence. Murmurings move amongst the gathered girls.

'Who'd have thought...'

'And her maintaining that superior attitude when all the time...'

'Thinking herself better than the rest of us...'

Fannie moves to snatch back the letter, and manages to break free of the fingers pinched around her arms, but the supervisor dodges her. Fury surges through her every nerve then, and she doesn't even think about what comes next. Her muscles act independently of her mind. Her right arm flies out to her side, she swings from her shoulder, and with all the might she can muster, she slaps the supervisor hard across her face.

The crack of it is repeated by the scowling rafters. It is accompanied by the collective gasp of the girls. And then, as anticipated, by the boot-steps of the foreman as he storms across the factory floor. Fannie feels the boards shifting beneath her feet, the wood springing with each thump. But she does not shrink. She will not. She finds the supervisor's eyes and, holding them, opens her mouth to a smile. However frightening this is, there is freedom in it, too. Fannie knows now that she will walk out of this factory today and never return, and the thought sends her soaring from terror to euphoria and back again.

'Don't imagine I didn't see that, you fucking madam.' He stops before her and jabs his fists against his hips. 'Collect your things and get out!'

Fannie spins on her heel. 'But...'

The foreman menaces her from a height of near six and a half feet. He is three times as wide as she. She cannot fight him.

And no, she finds, she will not beg him. She swallows the *please* which had been threatening her throat. The room is made suddenly hot by so many bodies: their gossiping, their belching, their yawns, their perspiration, their coughs. Fannie can feel droplets of these people wetting her skin, and she cannot stand it a second longer. She stops to retrieve nothing. She owns nothing of worth but her choices, and moment by moment, she is growing more convinced that something new lies ahead – a future she might take control of. A future in which she might mother her daughter again.

Without another word, she strides towards the door at the furthest end of the workroom. Beneath its heavy wood, a pale crack of daylight shows her the way. She does not glance back.

Letters

When she reaches the letter-writer's door, her bonnet ribbons are flying loose and her cheeks are as pink as her pale skin ever manages to flush. The instant she'd breathed the cold air outside the factory, she had lost the ability to ascend out of her fear towards hope. Her heart pounds so loudly it might set the ships anchored in the docks rocking.

'I'm closing up, Miss,' comes a gruff voice from behind the wood, just as her fingers find the handle.

'No!' Fannie shrieks. 'No, you can't be. You can't. I need just a few sentences. Please...'

The disembodied voice cuts her short.

'I've been here since six this morning, and I'll be here at the same time tomorrow. Come back then.'

'I can't!' Fannie lowers her forehead to the painted black wood and speaks into it. 'You see, my child is unwell, and she needs her medicine, and unless I promise to send the money...'

She slaps a flattened hand against the door, trying to force back her tears. The whack is answered at length by the clicking of a latch on the other side and the whine of the door swinging open by three mean inches. An eye appears in the gap: it is round and rheumy; the iris grey; the pupil clouded.

'I have to let them know I'll send the money.'

The eye closes as the head it belongs to nods in agreement.

'But quietly,' says the letter-writer, as he opens the door a couple of inches wider. 'I've been trying to lock up for over half an hour. I've a bed to get to, you know.'

'Thank you. Thank you,' Fannie breathes as she slips inside.

The letter-writer's office is a simple front hallway. It is around eight feet in length, and perhaps a tad over three feet wide. A panelled interior door of heavy oak, closed, separates the room from the rest of the house, though Fannie suspects the clag of cigarette smoke and stained ceilings extend throughout. Between the two doors sits a wide wooden bureau, scattered with loose sheets of paper and half-empty ink pots. It is tall enough to allow the letter-writer to work on his feet, negating the need for a chair, which would no doubt become wedged between the narrow walls. Or perhaps the intention was to discourage anyone from lingering here too long.

Fannie allows these thoughts to pass through her mind as she waits for the letter-writer to fumble about at his bureau, retrieve his pen, and angle it questioningly between his forefinger and thumb. The thoughts distract her from hysteria. She refuses to remember that she hasn't anything to pay the letter-writer with until the instant he turns to her and lifts his ashy eyebrows to indicate that she might start. She has been dismissed without pay. There is not a coin upon her person.

She rounds her lips, as though she is saying 'oh', but no sound issues. She pats at the pockets of her skirts, her faded coat. Her mouth gapes. Her face opens into dismay.

'Tomorrow, then,' grumbles the letter-writer.

Fannie nods. 'I'm sorry. Yes. Tomorrow.'

In a blink, she is outside again, and the streets are dark, and she doesn't know where to go. She cannot tramp about begging work at this caliginous hour. She cannot return to her lodgings and her bed without finding some way to post her letter. She cannot take a drink at a tavern alone; she cannot pay for a drink in any case.

Were it not so heavy with fear, the night would be beautiful. The morning mists have been shone away by a brilliant owl-eyed moon. The air is sharp and cold. The ground is beginning to glint with frost. It is one of those winter's nights that tightens your skin, waters your eyes, straightens your back. Fannie considers the row of lamps to her right, casting hoops of warm light onto the pavements, and begins to walk.

That summer, they walked the entire city, Fannie and her gentleman. In the stone-and-sapphire dawns, they took to the boatyards, to watch the shipbuilders bang and hammer and clank, to inhale the fresh seaweed stink and laugh at how much Fannie savoured it. In the slow-falling dusks, they strolled through the parks, where on every bench they found giggling couples, behind every gnarled tree trunk, a flushed and tangled pair. Everyone seemed to be courting. Fannie's gentleman blamed the weather. 'The heat,' he murmured, leaning into her neck. His words drifted on the tang of an early coffee. His plump lips were dry, slightly crusted. 'Come winter, you'll see, they'll all be shoving each other out.' Fannie shivered to think of any one of those smiling, petticoated girls trudging through the December snows, dirtying her hems, her arms wrapped not around her trembling body but around the fresh cleft at her middle. At sixteen, Fannie had never known heartbreak. Indeed, it was only during those three summer months that she had known love. But she had seen heartbreak: she had seen it fill a room with trinkets and jumble, and lock the door from the inside; she had seen it weaken the back and shoulders of a labouring man until he could no longer lift a spade; she had seen it starve a body to juts and bones. She grasped her gentleman's slender hand tighter.

'Shall we go as far as the lake?' she asked.

Along the paths and pavements, the lamps were already lit. Beyond the gnarled branches and thick leaves of the park oaks, the sky was fading to grape and lavender. It was too late, really, to venture further.

'Shall we go into the lake?' he returned, flashing a smile: neat teeth; a flick of pink tongue tip.

Fannie laughed. 'We can't.'

'We can. We can do anything we like. Don't you see, Fannie, we're entirely free, you and I.'

Lifting his arm, he spun her under it, as though they were partnered at a grand ball, and though Fannie smiled as he danced her about, and as they raced to the lake, and as they waded squealing in, she knew that the freedom was his alone. She hadn't the money to buy it, nor the position to demand it, nor the sex to expect it. Even then, she had known.

But wasn't she proud on that arm of his, listening to him talk of his studies at the university, and the vagaries of the law, and how he would one day take over his father's firm, and pretending, all the time, that she would still be standing alongside him when his future arrived?

Love, she knows, transforms even the most sensible people into fantasists.

She walks until she reaches the boatyards. She cannot say why, exactly, except perhaps that she is following the traces of her memory. Along the way, she stops at a merchant's office and begs a pen, a single sheet of paper, and a dip of ink. She is rewarded with three sheets of paper, together with the other implements, and bows her thanks to the apple-cheeked young clerk who helps her.

At the bridge, she stops under an umbrella of lamplight and places the papers down side by side on top of the balustrade. It is approaching seven o'clock and the streets are still busy with promenading merchants and sailors, factory workers and servants, carriage drivers and drunks and street sellers. The smell of roasting nuts and horse shit. The click of rich men's canes and the slap of poor boys' softened soles. Fannie bends her head against their footsteps, dips the pen into the ink pot, and begins.

I wil fech the muney.

She pauses. The unused ink drops onto the paper, leaving little black bursts around her words, like inverted stars. The letters she has shaped are overly large and childlike. She has no idea whether they are spelt correctly, and she is ashamed of herself. Why didn't she ask her gentleman to teach her, instead of so much cavorting and...? She knows, in truth, that she did not ask because she was embarrassed. More embarrassed even than she will be when this letter falls into the innkeeper's hands and she proves herself, once more, to be nothing but a silly girl caught out by flattering words and fancy ideas. The day she had delivered her daughter to the inn, she had travelled in borrowed clothes, a too-large wedding band hooked over her knuckle and a tale of a wounded husband on her lips. She doubted she had been convincing, but she had tried to gift her child a better story.

She tries again.

I can bring mor monee.

The stone beneath leaves bumps in the paper where she draws the pen across it. She stops and traces each collection of lines and points and flicks, comparing one sentence to the other. Neither is more or less correct to her eyes. *Munny*, she writes. *Muney. Monee. Monie.* There could be a thousand variations. They all look like a reflection of the sound to Fannie.

And if that is the case, she decides, then surely the innkeeper and his wife will see the sounds on the page, too, however poor her writing.

I wil bring mor munny. Plees do not stop the medisun. I wil duliver it myself. Plees.

She considers her letter thrice over, then dips her pen into the ink, blots it on the practice sheet, and holds it over the clean sheet of paper. So concentrated is she on the composition of her promise that she does not notice two ships nudge into the docks under the staring moon, or the swearing and sparking of the shipbuilders about their work, or the large, colourful woman who has stopped to watch her struggle to arrange one letter after another on her already crumpled paper.

'Seems to me you're grappling a little there, dear,' the woman says, past the exhaled smoke of a bitter cigar. Her voice is as rough as the rasp of wind-borne sand. 'Why not let me help you?'

Pausing, Fannie finds that her heart is thundering in her chest. She is panting and exhausted, as though she has been running over miles rather than attempting to construct simple sentences. Eventually, she lowers her pen and turns towards the woman, and then it is as though there is no city beyond her, no sky above. This stranger mutes the rest of the world and Fannie is rapt.

The ruckles around the older woman's eyes and lips direct Fannie to age her at perhaps fifty. She is short in stature, but in every other respect she is expansive: her hair is waist-length, deep auburn, and vaults apart from any sort of style as though repulsed by its attachment to a body; her skirts and petticoats are many layered and jut out in shuttlecock fashion; her shawls number perhaps five, all of differing bright shades, and are loosely thrown about her wide shoulders and enormous bosom.

'Why would you help me?' Fannie asks.

The woman smiles. 'I help wherever I can,' she replies. 'Especially when I see such a pretty young woman looking so lost. I'm everyone's mother around here. It's what they call me.'

'Mother?'

She nods.

'And you can write?'

She nods again. 'I can.'

Fannie is mesmerised by Mother's mouth. It has been painted in rich vermilion, but the lips beneath the paint are dry and cracked, and the colour has crept into the crevices of her wrinkles, so that Mother appears to be wearing her veins on the outside of her skin.

After a jot of hesitation, Fannie offers Mother the pen. The hand which receives it is plump and cold; the rings adorning every finger turn the flesh around them white. Fannie recognises the tightened bumps and bulges of rheumatism.

'Now, what do you want to say?'

Fannie begins, and as she speaks, she watches her words curl out across the page like the stems of blooming black flowers. It is magic, this act of translation.

'There,' Mother says, handing the paper back to Fannie. 'I'm sorry for your daughter. God willing she'll be well again soon.'

'Yes,' Fannie replies. The paper trembles in her grip. She studies the beautiful loops of Mother's writing, and then, with a jolt, realises that she cannot pay her, just as she could not pay the letter-writer, just as she will not make her rent this month if she cannot immediately secure another position. Tears clog her throat. 'I haven't...' Fannie begins. 'That is. I'll need to go home to get your payment.'

Mother waves her hand over her shoulder, as though she is batting away the incoming cloud. The bracelets at her wrist jangle; many but, to Fannie's eye, inexpensive. Mother, it seems, is something of an act. She has on the costume to prove it.

'I don't need it, child. Your daughter does.'

'But...'

'Will you go to her?'

Fannie presses her lips together and blinks.

'Ah. You can't,' Mother says.

'I lost my position today.'

'You'll find another.'

'Not without a recommendation... The foreman, he...'

Mother nods. 'I see.'

She sighs and shifts her cumbrous body so that she is looking out into the darkness. From this angle, her belly protrudes like the hull of a ship, and Fannie cannot help but imagine her the wild figurehead of a grand vessel. Queen of the high seas. Her hair strewn with seaweed, her shawls sailing behind her, her arms thrown wide as she guides her ship between rocks and over sandbanks. *Bring me in, fellows*, she would command, and every sailor aboard would obey without question, however hazardous the coast. This woman seems to Fannie somewhere between human and myth. She is not attractive, as such, but she is captivating.

'Listen,' Mother continues, though Fannie already is

listening. Mother's words are a mermaid's song. 'Start with your clothes and your hair.'

She turns back towards Fannie and, reaching out, teases the ends of her curls.

'If that's not enough, offer your teeth. Let me see.'

Mother grasps Fannie's cheeks in one hand and squeezes. Fannie bares her teeth.

'Ah, yes,' Mother continues. 'Fine teeth. The front two will sell.'

'But I can't...'

'You can, child. You'll do anything, won't you, to get your daughter better.'

Overhead, the moon eases out from behind a wispy swag of cloud and silvers the docks.

'Yes.' Fannie nods.

'Then if your clothes, your hair, and your teeth aren't enough, come back and find me. I'll have a position for you.'

'You will? I'm a hard worker, truly I am.'

Mother's hand rises to silence her. 'It won't be a position you'll want, child. Not a sweet girl like you. But if it becomes necessary... You'll find me here, every evening. Do you understand?'

Fannie pauses. The tightness across her chest persuades her that she does. 'I do,' she answers.

'Good.'

The two women clasp hands momentarily before Mother rotates slowly about and walks away. Or rather, sways. That, Fannie considers, is how she moves: as though she is being buffeted by a stiff cross-shore; as though she is riding the swelling pitch-and-pale waves. In motion, she seems larger still, and Fannie wonders how she will shimmy through the small gap between the two grounded rowing boats she is approaching.

'Land ahoy,' Fannie murmurs.

In the cold, clear night, her voice must carry, because Mother turns. 'Land ahoy,' she repeats.

Fannie feels her colour rise. How quickly she ruins her chances. Perhaps the foreman was right to dismiss her. Her head and ears throb as she waits for Mother to chastise her, but the older woman only opens her mouth, tosses back her head, and laughs. Her spine arches. Her breath plumes upwards. 'That's funny,' she wheezes. 'Land ahoy. Ha! I see what you mean.'

When she turns from Fannie again, she lifts her arms out to both sides, her shawls held between her fingers so that, in silhouette, she really does resemble the retreating stern of a ship, and glides away. Fannie releases an unexpected burst of laughter.

'Now go home, child,' Mother calls as she departs.

And Fannie, her letter held against her chest, obeys. She will count all the money in her pillowcase, send it to the innkeeper and, tomorrow, she will do better. No more labouring over stitches for pittance. No more holding her breath as the foreman passes and hoping that he will not touch her. No more enduring the cruel words of the factory girls. No more wrapping her bleeding fingertips inside her gloves so that she does not stain the fabric. She will make her own way. And she will earn enough to pay for her daughter's medicine. And she will go to her, and administer it herself, and nurse her until she is better.

Though life has always insisted otherwise, the arrival of Mother has spun a spell to make Fannie believe she can do anything she desires.

Ashes

Her room, when she shoulders open the swollen door and steps inside, is stale, cold, and dim. The only illumination is that which chances weakly through the dirty windowpane from the street lamp on the opposite pavement. The temperature has been dropping steadily all evening and she thinks that perhaps the city will see snow tonight. She would like to sit at the window and watch the flakes waltz downwards to gather on the roof tiles and the chimney tops, in the twisted branches of the elms, in the manes of waiting cab horses, along the kerbs and in the storm drains. She would like the city to be made brighter. Striking a match, she holds it to the candle she keeps beside the door and, by its guttering glow, moves to the fire. She has had no wood for days and she has resorted to pulling the straw from her mattress and huddling close to the quick-dying flames for a few fleet minutes before throwing herself beneath her sheets and drawing her limbs in tight. She had not realised her bed could grow so chill when her gentleman had lain in it.

Tonight, she uses the sheet of practice letter paper to start the flames sputtering, then retrieves the money from her pillowcase and, spreading it on the boards before the fire, begins to count. It takes less than a minute for her to reach her total: two-thirds of what she must find by the week's end.

Slumping back onto her haunches, Fannie stares into the fire. Soon, in the ripple and snap of the flames, she fancies she sees a pair of dancing girls, turning pirouettes on tiptoe and whirling with laughter. Perhaps her daughter plays with her adopted sisters so, she thinks. She watches until the happy pair transform into an untamed mare, throwing up her hooves and whipping her tail before launching into a gallop. Fannie watches and watches. A blackening fragment of paper becomes a soaring nighthawk. A dwindling flame leaves a shadow puppet, finally cut loose from its strings, on the wall. Her imagination has always been her downfall. Wasn't her mother forever warning her against dreaming into adulthood without proper plans to follow? Didn't her gentleman tease her, for the way she cast her ideas out onto the bare floorboards of her room and spoke them into life for him?

Just there, beside her cracked washbasin, she had word-painted her future self, binding a baby snug inside a clean towel and lullabying it to sleep. Here, before the fire, she had dropped her gentleman to his knee and had him lift a ring for her consideration. In the bare middle of the room, their steps echoing over the place where a rug had once lain, she had pictured them dancing the winter nights warm.

Her gentleman had vanished before the first frosts fell.

Within half an hour, the fire is dying. Through her tears,

Fannie watches the cinders dull and wane. Outside, the wind rises to rattle the windowpane and, on its whistle, she hears Mother's words repeated back to her. *Start with your clothes and your hair.* Fannie has no clothes to offer: one pair of scuffed brown boots, her darned stockings, two simple dresses, a single pair of gloves, her blue bonnet, and her faded coat. But her hair.

Standing, she rushes to the mirror, grabs her brush, and pulls it through the curls the tussle at the factory had tangled. She grits her teeth against the rasp of it as she feels strands snap free. It does not matter. It will not matter. By the crowing of dawn, it will no longer be hers.

The Slums

Slamming the door behind her, Fannie stumbles down the staircase and lurches out onto the cobbles. The street is narrow. Whenever a horse and cab pass down it, pedestrians are forced to lift their hems and slop into the mess of leaves and mire which gathers along its edges; there are no pavements here, in the poorer part of the city. But now it is quiet, and Fannie is able to stride down the middle of the street undisturbed. The memory of ballerinas – straight as an honest look, delicate as lily petals – holds her every muscle suitably taut, and she glides as gracefully as a swallow over the uneven ground.

An argument hammers against the pane of an upstairs window and Fannie glances up to see the shadow of a man standing braced as his wife pounds at his chest with her fists. Three or four strikes later, she collapses into him and allows herself to be held. Fannie moves on. She knows which part of the city she must visit for a transaction such as this. She must go beyond the docks and then south, into the slums. There, everything is for sale.

She's visited only once before. With her gentleman. When they had ventured out in search of Turkish opium, which, her gentleman told her, had the strongest hallucinogenic properties. 'For pleasure,' he'd winked, and she had clung to him as the slum dwellers had reached out for her hands, her hair. *So pale*, they'd pleaded. *So fair*. As though all they were in want of was simple sanitation; as though they weren't already starved to bones and mad with it.

In the slums, she knows, her gold curls will fetch a pretty price.

The smell reaches out for her while she still has the noise of the docks – the heaving ships, the hollering sailors – in her ears. It is a tacky smell, so thick with alcohol and urine and tobacco smoke and despair that Fannie presses her hand over her mouth for fear that it will work its way into her body. It has a taste, this smell. It is leathery and bitter over her tongue. Fannie finds she cannot swallow it. She steps slower, recalling the hollow-eyed beggars, the skull-and-skin children. She would turn back, were it not for her daughter's laughter echoing through her memory. Two years now since Fannie waved her off into a better life. Two years since she has listened to her sing. Two years since she has held another person. And how she wishes she had someone to hold now, as she crosses into the slums, and the mounds of muck banked up against the stonework of the buildings reveal themselves to have faces, hands, feet, hearts. It is corporeal, the need she has to be held. It is more than a want. It is the throb of a wound, or the thrust of a cough up the throat. It is as unstoppable and necessary as all those bodily happenings, and the lack of it leaves Fannie cold. Always cold. The beggars she is walking by must surely share in this with her, and because and in spite of the fact, she wants to stop and talk with every one of them. To find out their stories.

She lifts her chin higher. She cannot let herself be deterred. It is Wednesday night. She has only until Friday to find the rest of the sum the innkeeper has asked for.

The bellowing of the hawkers directs her through the labyrinth of streets, and finally she enters an alleyway lined by shawled women carrying baskets and vials, jars and barrels: jellied eels, beaded necklaces, seashells, apples, scarves, glass eyes, breads, tobacco pipes, spirits, herbs, curiosities suspended in vinegar, mismatched boots, brooches, vanity mirrors, bed linens, fortunes. All are coated in a fine layer of smut. Above, across the seven feet or so which separate the alleyway's two teetering walls, white sheets have been hung. Weathered to a dirty cream and sagging, they reveal only three slender sickles of sky. Without sight of the moon or stars, it seems darker here.

'What can we do you for, miss?' a woman croaks. 'Some rouge for those pale cheeks, perhaps?'

'No, thank you,' Fannie replies.

'Something to fill your belly then?' says another voice behind her.

Fannie spins around. 'Oh, no. Thank you. I...'

'I know what you need,' claims a slim girl with startling, bright-green eyes, who is suddenly upon her. 'It's a pretty ornament you want, for that lovely hair of yours.'

Filthy faces loom towards her, crowding closer and closer, their fetid breaths clouding the way through. Hands pluck at her skirt. Fingers pinch the skin of her arms. She whirls about once, twice, then grasps the green-eyed girl's shoulder. The girl's eyes constrict in defiance. *I'll give you nothing for nothing*, says the tightening of her jaw. 'My hair,' Fannie breathes. 'Do you know where I might sell it?'

The girl, realising that Fannie is almost as desperate as she, shrinks by an inch or two. 'At the end,' she says, indicating the way with a dip of her head, 'turn right. Second door on the left.'

'Thank you,' Fannie calls as she rushes away. She does not want to stay here a moment longer than she must. A cold dread is shivering across her shoulders. She feels constantly that someone or something is about to touch her back.

At the end of the alleyway, she puts a hand to the stone to steady herself as she wheels around the corner. The hand comes away deep green and slimy. She stops, lifts her skirt, and wipes it clean against her stocking – the easiest item to wash. Then, straightening up and settling herself with a deep breath, she steps forward and raps on the second door.

It is a small, wooden arch – any grown adult would have to duck to move through it – and Fannie wonders at what kind of person resides within.

Soon she is summoned inside by a guttural, 'Enter.'

Pushing open the door, Fannie shuffles into heavy gloom. In a far corner, a candle is lit, but it illuminates only a tiny wedge of the room. A bulky figure waits in a wingback chair, which the candle shows to be deep crimson and torn. Fannie squints at the person, but can make out only a large gathering of skirts, and a pair of plump, aged hands locked across a belly.

'Hello, dear.'

Fannie's blood chills at the realisation of who she is standing before.

'I hadn't expected you so soon, but I'm always ready for a visitor.'

'But you... Do you live here?'

'Oh no,' says Mother. 'I visit occasionally, that's all. To see how business is doing. Now, we're shearing you today, are we? You'll want to keep the teeth a little longer, I should say.'

At this, Mother pushes herself upwards with a long groan. Turning her colossal back on Fannie, she fidgets with a lamp for a trice then, lifting it, shambles across the room. The shifting light swings over a wooden ladderback chair, placed baldly in the middle of the space, and beside it, a long wooden sideboard, scattered with every sort of implement. Blunt-ended scissors, hook-ended scissors, forceps, pliers, needles with rounded eyes in place of points, razor blades. None is clean enough to glint, but their rusted shapes are altogether discernible as Mother suspends the lamp above them and, putting a forefinger to her lips, deliberates over her tool of choice.

'Is it a difficult decision?' Fannie asks, careful to keep her voice from fluttering.

Mother's body remains bent over her tools, but her head swivels in Fannie's direction. 'Pah!' she laughs. 'Not so very difficult, no. I was just trying to decide which would allow me closest to the skin without ruining the curl. What do you think?' She grins. Not menacingly, but – it seems to Fannie – honestly. After all, she is only making her living. It is not so very different from sitting in a row of factory girls and stitching fabric to make rich women look pretty. Mother will make a poor woman look ugly instead, but it is a transaction all the same. A service. A necessary exchange. Her looks for her daughter's health. It is not such a difficult decision.

Fannie moves to the sideboard and pauses fleetingly before plucking up a medium-sized pair of scissors with a point which tapers into invisibility. They are lighter than expected.

'Small enough to crop close to the skull,' she explains. 'Sharp enough to take the hair away cleanly.'

'Well,' Mother croons, 'you do surprise me, child. So calm. So definite. Are you certain you are only an out-of-work seamstress?'

'I'm certain I'm a great deal more,' Fannie replies, standing to her fullest height, which, while not significant, exceeds Mother's by some three or four inches.

Mother rests her weight against the sideboard and crosses her arms, with some difficulty, over her brimming bust. 'Is that so? And what more might you be, tell me?'

'Well, I was once a dancer with the Royal Ballet,' Fannie says, inventing an entirely new existence for herself in a breath. Why not? She has no life of her own to claim anymore. There is nothing to stop her rewriting her past. So willing is she suddenly to convince herself that she was once a completely different girl, that she almost lifts her arm to demonstrate some swishing movement she could not possibly know the name of. Mother's collusion in the game keeps her from feeling foolish.

'Oh, yes?' says Mother. 'Go on.'

'And after that, I rode out horses for the Queen.'

'For the Queen, no less! And then you decided to become a seamstress.'

'In a manner of speaking,' Fannie replies, tilting her chin. 'Decisions are not always made by one person alone.'

'And yet they must often be borne by one person alone,' Mother muses.

Fannie nods her head slowly. 'Yes, I suppose you are right. But I shall not suffer for mine. I have decided that I will wear my cropped scalp proudly.'

Mother's smile drops. She touches a gentle hand to Fannie's shoulder. 'Let's see, shall we?'

At Fannie's throat, something thickens. She gulps it away. 'Perhaps,' she begins, a little louder than is necessary in the cave-like room, 'I could become a nun. I hear a cold head is important to the job.'

'Are you sure you could suit the habit?' Mother asks.

Fannie gives a small shrug. 'They are a little drab, but I've worn this coat for so long, I'm sure I'd welcome the change.'

Mother indicates the chair, and Fannie obliges, noting as she sits how hard the wood is against her buttocks. Likely, she has shed more weight. At the thought, her stomach grumbles for a hot baked potato; the crisped skin is her favourite. When she last ate, she couldn't say.

'It's a brave choice,' Mother mumbles, gathering up Fannie's hair. As she plaits it – so it doesn't fall loose when it is cut, Fannie assumes – Fannie stays silent. Her hair has always been her greatest beauty. She knew that long before her gentleman uttered the words. But it is not the beauty of it she mourns, as Mother cuts the air to ensure the snap of her scissors is sharp enough. It is that her hair, whatever its shade or curl, is hers and hers alone. It is a part of what makes her Fannie. Were there some way to paint her irises brown, or make her ears smaller, or widen her smile, Fannie would not subscribe to it. God or nature or chance has made a decision as to the curves and colours which make her up, and the world would not know her if they were to change. She would not know herself.

While Mother plaits and plaits, she hums softly. Fannie closes her eyes to the lullaby, realising that it is the very same one she used to sing to her daughter. She had thought she had invented it, but she must only have learnt it somewhere. How else would Mother know it too? Mother loops one layer of hair over another, rhythmically, humming, and Fannie's breathing starts to slow. She sways slightly with the melodic lilts of Mother's voice. Her head begins to nod; the room grows warmer around her; she hides in the dark behind her eyelids and, for the first time in many months, her shoulders lower, her stomach slackens, and she drops towards a dreamless sleep. Fannie longs for rest which is not haunted by her daughter's skipping laugh, or the phantom grasp of her gentleman's hands over hers as he moves against her.

The calm is broken by Mother's voice and Fannie's eyes peel open again.

'Last chance, child,' she says. 'Are you certain about this?'

Fannie nods. 'Yes.'

Bending forwards, Mother swings her head around to bring herself nose to nose with Fannie. 'Yes?'

'Yes,' Fannie replies, but the word is little more than a tremor.

Mother's eyebrows lift. 'Yes?' she asks again.

'Yes,' Fannie says, firmer this time.

'Yes?' Mother bellows, gripping the roots of Fannie's hair suddenly and wrenching back her head. Something near the top of Fannie's spine pops. The base of her skull cracks against the top of the chair. She tenses, making sure not to emit a cry of pain. Strength is what Mother wants her to demonstrate, she knows. Determination. And Fannie has enough of that to tear out every last strand of her hair with her own hands should she need to.

She fixes her eyes unblinking on the damp-blackened ceiling and the flicker of candlelight over it, wraps her hands tight around the splintered arms of the chair, and bawls, 'Do it, Mother!' The command echoes off the bare stone walls. 'Do it!' Her voice seems to shift the stonework. All around her trembles. Dust suffuses the room. 'Now!' she screams, and whatever it is that controls her voice vibrates hideously in her throat, threatening to snap. An unexplained agony is pulsing through her body. Fury, she supposes. Fury that she has been reduced to making this grubby transaction; that all the while her gentleman has more money than he could ever need; that her daughter is sick and she cannot hold her to her breast; that Mother will likely pay her a pittance for her beautiful hair; that her hair will not be enough. Fannie fears she might rupture she is so angry. But who would care for her daughter then? Who would buy the medicine her sweet girl needs if not Fannie? There is no choice but this. And yet, she does not have to accept it quietly. Stare set on the ceiling, she opens her mouth as wide as her jaw will allow and she screams.

She is silenced only by the first snip of the scissors, which seems to sound louder than any bedlam her lungs can produce. Her tears had sprung from her scream but she refuses to snivel or whimper as Mother lifts each plait away from her head and – snip – shears her like a common herd animal. Fannie lifts her chin and clamps her lips against the quivering. It is only hair. Only hair. No – it is more than that. It is her daughter's saviour.

'Mother,' she says.

'Yes, child.'

'I don't want to keep my teeth.'

Blood

There is one thing Fannie feels she knows without a doubt, as she scutters away from Mother's, her mouth swilling with blood, and it is that she has never been properly loved. Her gentleman had enjoyed the shell of her well enough. Her parents, before their deaths, had admired her with a sort of detached approval – largely, she supposes, because her manners were adequate enough to do them proud in sophisticated company. An aunt of hers had shown interest for a while, hoping Fannie might become a teacher at her small, underfunded schoolhouse. But none had loved her in a simple, truthful way. None had wanted her for what she was, only what she could offer them. None, should they pass by her now, would gather her scalped and toothless form to their chest and hold her while she wept.

And so, she concludes, she must not weep.

She hurries on, the knitted scarf Mother has loaned her wrapped tight about her head and pinched beneath her chin. Past the crones flogging their wares beneath a canopy of sullied sheets. Past the docks, with its fleet of slumber-swayed ships, and the furrowed reflection of the moon pointing far out to sea. Through the sleeping streets with their fading lamps and their sneaking tree branches. Now and then, she stops to spit clots of blood onto the pavements, straightening up and wiping her mouth before she hears the revolting splatter.

However ugly she now is, she need not lower herself to bad habits. She swallows as much of the blood as she can.

As she passes the corner she would need to take to return to her room, she catches sight of a strange movement in the street ahead. Fluid. Confident. Stalking. A sudden flick of soft-grey tail confirms that it is the cat she saw this morning. Though surely it was not only this morning that she had walked to the factory? Already, she is a different woman.

And she wonders, as she begins to follow the cat, whether this woman will have a better chance at life than did her predecessor. With no hair, and no teeth, will she be taken on her merit rather than judged on her appearance? Might she, after all, be taken seriously? Fannie stifles a snort of bitter laughter. A picture of the dock women has entered her mind. The ships come and the ships go, but those women only ever make it as far as the end of the jetty. They are trapped. Crowded together on the rotting planks. Reaching out. And never travelling anywhere.

What it would be, Fannie considers, to leap aboard one of those ships and be washed out on the next tide. Oh, she would gladly transform into a wooden figurehead, bound to the prow of a galleon, if she could live out the rest of her days with her arms outstretched and her skirts billowing about her, the restless water spitting at her feet and the salt wind scudding her cheeks. She would relinquish womanhood for such freedom.

Perhaps that was what she had seen in Mother at first glance, when she had imagined her like a ship: freedom.

Fannie pays little attention to their direction as she trails the cat through the empty city. She is captivated by her movement: the way she slinks, stops, shifts her whiskers towards possible danger, steals lower, pads on. She is the image of elegance, this cat. Though Fannie would swear her silvery fur is a touch thinner than it was this morning, that her tail is a deal less fluffed. She would think the animal had been caught in a rainstorm, except that she knows no rain has fallen today. Some disgruntled servant, then, has thrown a bucket of water over the poor thing for thieving from the kitchens. But when the cat pauses and Fannie grows closer, she sees that she is wrong. The cat is not wet; she has simply lost something of her lustre.

At a bench positioned beneath a failing lamp, Fannie crouches down, reaches out a tentative hand, and rubs her thumb and forefinger together to call the animal to her.

'Pss, pss, pss,' she hisses. Even this small sound is difficult without her two front teeth. *Pth, pth, pth.*

Maintaining a carriage length's distance, the cat sits down and stares, unblinking, at Fannie. A flick of the left ear. Two more. A whip of the tail.

'Come along, cat. I won't hurt you.' The words are distorted. Thicker than they ought to be.

The cat extends her front legs, drops her shoulders, and lifts her rump into a long stretch. Her tail trembles from root to tip, as though expelling some stress or rage. Then she relaxes and struts in Fannie's direction.

Fannie's desperation to touch her is childlike. She can hardly fathom the intensity of the urge, other than to suppose that, for want of human interaction, a cat might suffice. She needs only to touch and be touched. She holds her breath. She turns her hand over and offers a palm.

The cat, perhaps sensing her worth, lowers her head and shoves her soft grey skull into Fannie's hand. Fannie turns her hand over and feels the tuck and spring of small ears as the cat glides against the pressure of her touch, then the neat protrusion of her withers, each knuckle-like bump of her spine, and finally the tapering branch of her tail. Beneath her fur, she is little more than a skeleton. Fannie fancies she could stroll through the slums without tempting anyone to make a meal of her over an open fire.

'I hope you're not hungry,' Fannie says. 'I don't have anything to offer you.'

The cat, feeling her tail released, coils about and repeats the movement in the opposite direction. Head, withers, back, tail. Fannie counts the knots of her spine. She reaches seven before the cat's undulations shift her attention. Back and forth the cat goes, ducking her head, arching her back. The simple exchange is hypnotically calming. Beneath Fannie's cold hands, the cat is unspoilt velvet. She imagines Mother would covet her as a stole.

'But I wouldn't let that happen,' Fannie assures the unknowing cat. 'You're too beautiful for such a grisly end.' *Grithly*, comes the sound. The cat will understand.

When the cramping at her knees becomes too much, Fannie tips onto her side and rests her back against the seat of the bench. The sculpted iron is even colder than the pavement, but Fannie leans into it all the same. She measures its frosty bar between her shoulder blades and concludes that she is sitting straight enough. She lengthens her neck. A swan, she thinks, even without my feathers. A dancer, even with no music.

The cat steps onto the fan of her skirts, kneads the faded fabric a little, then curls herself up like a moon shell and tucks into sleep.

Fannie gives a light laugh. 'You don't mind what I look like, do you?' she says and, taking her cue from the cat, she bundles Mother's scarf under her head and promptly falls into sleep, where all her imaginings brighten into life and she runs through fallen autumn leaves with her daughter, and the cat dashes ahead of them, and she knows with a deep aching certainty that should they choose to, the three of them could simply sprout wings and fly away.

Cockcrow

First light tilts over the city with the birds, the colour of peaches and honey, and colder than dread. Two or three miles away, the muted rumpus of the docks rises with the fog, sending the hollers of departing sailors over the rooftops to wane amongst the smoking chimneys and the frosted slates. Fannie wakes, stiff and slow and shivering. Before she moves her feet, she checks the place where the cat had lain. Her skirt is rumpled, and the fabric slightly darker where the cold has not settled over it, but the cat is nowhere to be seen. Fannie looks up and down the cobbled street to orientate herself. She needs to get home. She needs to gather her money and send it all to the innkeeper. She needs to wash and change her dress and arrange a scarf over her shorn hair so that she might look presentable enough to seek a new position.

I am theeking a pothition, she will say, and her ruined mouth will be enough to get her turned away at the door.

Rolling out her shoulders, her wrists, her ankles, Fannie stands. As she does, she realises that she is directly opposite the letter-writer's house. Without another thought for her thawing muscles, she strides towards his door, dragging the money Mother gave her from her pocket as she goes.

Forming a tight fist, she hammers at the black paint. The flakes of older, peeled paint beneath the new layer make sharp little dents in her bunched skin.

'You said you would be here at six,' she yells.

She hears it back.

You thaid you would be here at thix.

A moment later, she hears a shuffling, the click of the door being unlatched. 'I'm here. I'm here,' comes the scratchy voice. 'Can a man not...? Oh.' He stops, the door open just far enough to show Fannie a narrow wedge of his shocked face. His voice softens. 'What happened to you, girl?'

Fannie straightens up. 'I got the money,' she replies.

He pauses, nods slowly. She hears him exhale. 'You did. Then you best come inside. We've a letter to write.'

'I've got my letter, too,' she says, clutching at her skirts again, thrusting her hand into each pocket until she finds – 'Here!' – the page she had dictated to Mother. 'I have the most of it in any case. I just need a little adding. Please.'

The letter-writer nods again, then moves aside for her to step through the doorway. She shoves the door shut too heavily behind her and winces at the slam. The letter-writer does not react. She notices, as he returns to his bureau and begins the drawn-out procedure she witnessed yesterday – searching for his pen, discovering it, angling it just so between his thumb and forefinger – that he is older than she had supposed him during her previous visit. His back is rounded like a bear's. His features pincer over a delicate pair of reading glasses. There is a visible tremor in his writing hand.

Fannie flattens the rumpled letter on the bureau and, standing at his shoulder, says, 'Please add, "Here is the sum you require for this week. More will follow on Friday."'

The old man scrawls her words across the page and then, setting down his pen and straightening up, turns to look square into her face.

'Indulge me a moment, if you will,' he says quietly. 'I see the situation you're caught in.' He indicates the waiting page. 'But there has to be a better way.' Kindness beads at the corners of his eyes.

Fannie shows him a sad smile. 'There is no *quicker* way, sir.'

The letter-writer nods in that slow, considered way he has. He lifts her letter and folds it into an envelope. 'No charge for this,' he says, holding it out to her.

'But, I—'

He waves her protest away. 'No charge,' he says again. 'For this, or any other letter you might need to send to or regarding your daughter. Only promise that you'll come back to me.'

Fannie eyes the dividing door, wondering if the letter-writer has a wife shut away in there. She wonders if he has anyone at all. He seems to her to wear that stale smell of loneliness.

'Will you promise?'

Fannie retrieves the letter and clutches it to her chest. 'I will.'

'Might I ask your age?' the letter-writer continues, shuffling some papers around on his bureau now. Lifting an ink pot. Moving it an inch. Setting it down again.

'Twenty-one, sir.'

'Ah.' The letter-writer nods again. 'I had a daughter once,' he says as he turns to let himself through the hall door and back into his private rooms. 'Now,' he calls over his shoulder, 'I'll expect you tomorrow morning.'

Yes, Fannie thinks, as she watches his slim shoulders disappear behind the door. And what will I have resorted to by then?

Demands

It is not often that Fannie's landlady is to be found loitering near the entranceway of the building she rents, room by room, to Fannie, an old dockworker with a bent spine, a middle-aged woman who is forever in her nightgown, a tense young couple with a sickly baby who cries from midnight till four o'clock every morning, and a sprightly lad of indeterminate employment who cannot be more than fifteen. It is not often she is seen at all, unless the rent is due. Which is not until Friday. Tomorrow.

'Good morning,' Fannie says as she approaches, standing as tall as she can and hoping she has wiped all the blood splatter from her lips.

'Good God!' replies the landlady, her hand springing to her mouth as though to protect herself from a contagion. 'Were you attacked?' Her small, neat eyes narrow in confusion. Fannie can see her itching to take a step backwards, but, to her credit, she stands her ground.

'No, madam,' Fannie answers. She offers no further explanation. 'Have you come for the rent?'

'No. I...' The landlady struggles to regain her bearing.

A fist of fear clenches in Fannie's stomach: how terrible must she look, for the landlady to be this disturbed?

'I assure you I am unhurt,' Fannie tries. It is not true. Her jaw smarts from having been forced open for so long. Her bones throb from having the teeth dragged and twisted and yanked from them. Fannie hadn't imagined a tooth could be so difficult to dislodge.

The landlady flinches, realising perhaps that she is being rude, and gives a small shake of her head. Her bonnet ribbons shimmy. 'No. I ... I will come for the rent on Friday as usual. I have a letter for you.' She rummages inside the breast of her velveteen coat and extracts a small envelope.

The fist in Fannie's stomach clenches tighter. Her name is the only word she can read on the front, but she recognises the script, and who else would she be receiving a letter from in any case? It is bad news. She knows it. It has been only days since the last.

'Would you read it for me?' Fannie asks quietly.

'Certainly.' The landlady turns the envelope over and begins to peel it open. The ease with which the lip unsticks betrays the fact that it has already been opened once. 'Should we go inside?'

Fannie shakes her head. 'Here is just fine.'

As the landlady pretends to scan the page and clears her throat, Fannie concentrates on the drip-drip of the frost melting down the drainpipe beside the door and forming a puddle on the cobbles beneath. By this evening, she thinks, that puddle will be a solid slick of ice.

'The child,' the landlady begins, at a whisper, 'grows sicker. The cost of medicine rises day on day. We will require twice what you sent last week.'

'This is why you came,' Fannie says.

Beneath her pretty bonnet and stiffened ringlets, the landlady has the decency to blush. 'There have been many demands. I wondered how much longer you would be able to afford the rent. I am sorry for your daughter, Fannie, but—'

'I have never missed a payment,' Fannie interrupts.

'And what has that cost you?' the landlady replies, unable to resist taking another glance at Fannie's cropped head, the jabs of blunted hair just visible beneath the hood of her scarf. 'I have already found another tenant. There is a young man ready to take the burden off your back, should you be ready to ... move on to another abode.'

The morning chill hits Fannie anew. It is *her* room. Her own. Inside it hangs the stitched portière she used to swish across to cocoon herself and her gentleman within their fantasies. Inside it is the bed where her gentleman made love to her and where, months after he'd gone, she'd lain back and bitten through the sheets as she'd delivered her daughter alone. She cannot give it up. And yet, without the rent to pay...

'I'll pay up until the end of the week and be gone before,' she says, and, without another word, she spins around and runs into the still-breaking dawn, her scarf and her skirts streaming behind her.

The innkeeper requires twice what she sent last week – an impossible sum. She knows now where she must go.

The Docks

Fannie has never ventured beyond the safety of the street lamps and down into the smoky, steel light of the docks before. No girl would be daft enough to do so alone. But today, she has little choice. She lifts her skirts by a careful inch as she descends, and drops them as soon as she reaches the bottom of the ladder, aware, as ever, of the roaming eyes of passing men. Brushing her hands over her hips, she straightens up and turns to confront the place.

At water level, it is a muddle of steps and piers, sails and pulleys. It creaks and shifts. Morning is still reaching for the topmost masts of the ships moored here overnight, casting a confusion of shadows over the jetty Fannie walks tentatively along. The damp, slatted wood gives a little beneath her boots. The effect is of being at sea, she imagines, though she has never been at sea herself and has nothing to compare the unbalanced feeling to. The tang of boxed spices prickles in her nose. The warmer scent of tea leaves settles on her tongue. The docks taste of salt and unknown places, and Fannie breathes in deeply, wanting to hold all those exotic flavours inside her body. The body, she suspects, she is about to give up.

As she moves further into the warren of walkways and between the looming bellies of the ships, she is met by the silhouettes of men, striding and lugging and smoking and chatting. When they pass, their steps sure and heavy, she drops her head, expecting a leer or crude words. But for the first time since her adolescence, none of them looks at her. No smirks. No grasping hands. No slathering lips. For a moment, she had forgotten the decision she was forced to reach last night, but their indifference reminds her. Without her hair and her teeth, she has been made invisible. No longer can she barter with her gold curls. No more can she use her beauty as a mask. She will have to find a new way to exist in the world.

And perhaps, because of that, the position Mother offered her by the bridge will now be closed. Or wider open.

She lifts her chin and attempts to walk proudly past the dockworkers who ignore her. She feels safer somehow, knowing that they will not desire her – that what they will see as she passes, wrapped in her scarf, is at best an old spinster and at worst a wandering witch. She notices a darkened archway up ahead, cut out of the huge stone structure which holds up the streets above, and steps towards it. It is out of the dark they always come, when she watches them from the bridge.

'Mother?' she calls as she approaches. A puddle of stagnant water seeps from the blackness of the archway. In its greasy surface, the dulled reflection of the hem of her blue dress and the increasingly indigo sky. Leaning forward, Fannie peers into the shadows, but she can make out nothing but the nearby drip of water. From within comes the echo of a far-off giggle.

'Mother?' she calls louder. Her voice rattles against the stonework.

'There's no need to bellow, child.'

Fannie spins around to find Mother at her back.

'Where did you...?'

Mother flaps her hand to dismiss the question. 'I take it you're considering my offer,' she says. 'You want to come aboard the good ship Mother.' Her head drops back to better release her hooting laugh. Fannie gets a flash of her crescent of upper teeth: three of them are gold. 'Land ahoy! Remember! You'll need your humour here. Come.'

Mother wraps a strong arm around Fannie's shoulder and steers her through the archway. Immediately the daylight is blotted out and Fannie, unsure of her step, lifts her feet too high before her, like a child or a blind person. Mother, though, is confident of her way. They take an abrupt left into warmer air. On the inward curve of the wall ahead, an unseen fire throws a dancing, beacon-like glow. Fannie widens her eyes, but still cannot discern the detail of her surroundings. A few paces later, they come upon a smaller doorway: a crudely-made hole in the wall, supported by three thick beams of mismatched timber; it tilts to the right slightly.

'In you go, then,' Mother says and Fannie, heart pounding now, complies and ducks through the doorway.

Her entrance silences the clowning of the three girls gathered around the fire. They turn their heads to stare at her, but not their shoulders or their backs, which stay positioned against her, like shields. Fannie takes in their various states of undress.

On the left, a striking redhead reclines along a tattered old chaise longue, her slender legs stretched out so that her heels rest on the heap of chopped logs beside the fire. She looks unblinking over her shoulder at Fannie, her right hand plucking at the strap of her thin, silk slip. Fannie can hear the cracking of the material as the threads split, then the softened snap of the released strap meeting the skin of the girl's shoulder: it is like the tocking of a clock.

Framed by the lucency of the flames, her hand draped over the redhead's ankle, sits an older woman – perhaps thirty-five – whose bared upper arms are dimpled and bruised. Her tangle of tawny curls is piled high on her skull, revealing a twist at the top of her spine which Fannie supposes must be a birth defect.

To her right, a torn stocking dangling from her fingers and one foot hooked up on a side table, stands the youngest of the three – a willow of a girl, with gently flowing limbs and the poise of a trapeze artist.

'Say hello to our new girl,' Mother instructs them, patting Fannie on the rump as she sidles past. Fannie tries not to flinch against the sting, but she suspects she gives herself away a little.

'Looking like that?' the younger girl sneers, glancing up and down the length of Fannie's body. It is apparent, even from across the room, that the girl stands a head taller than she.

'Hair grows back,' Mother retorts. 'As well you know.'

At this, the girl drops her sneer and plucks up the ends of her own sleek brown tresses.

'And Fannie's is the most beautiful pale gold. You know how much the customers like the fair-haired girls.'

'Don't we just,' replies the redhead, tossing her own locks over her shoulder. 'I've tried all sorts to lighten mine, but there are only so many lemons anyone can bear to squeeze over their scalp.' She touches a palm to her crown, as though she can still feel a smarting there. 'And I didn't see a bit of difference.'

Fannie idles in the middle of the room, unsure what to say or do. She cannot take a seat without moving one of the girls aside, but she longs to move closer to the fire. The doorway without a door; the damp stone walls of the tunnels without; all convince her that her very bones are trembling.

She shivers at the sudden brush of Mother's breath against her neck.

'No one here will force you, child,' she murmurs. Her words smell like coffee and vinegar. 'But you'd make a good buck, and fast too, and this lot would help you out. They like to play at barking, but they're sweet as kittens really. And they all act out their parts, keep the punters interested. There are worse bunches to fall in with.'

'What parts?' Fannie asks.

'Well.' Mother raises an eyebrow, gives her bust the subtlest of jiggles. 'You know.' She points out each woman in turn, moving from left to right, as Fannie's regard had. 'The rebel. The lover. The virgin. Every customer—'

'But,' Fannie interrupts unthinkingly, 'what about your names?'

'Our names were the first things they took from us,' the lover replies.

Mother huffs affectedly and continues. 'Every customer has his preferences.'

'Tiresome as that gets,' the lover puts in, holding her tucked hand up to inspect her dirty nails and picking at something she finds there. 'You'd think they were at the theatre, some of them, oohing and aahing the way they do. Christ, this is an easy life compared to some, Fannie... It was Fannie, wasn't it?' She turns but does not rise from the bench. Fannie nods. 'I mean, once you get over the initial shock of the thing, it's really not so bad.'

'We'll look after you, Fannie,' the rebel puts in, with what Fannie thinks – hopes – is kindly resignation. 'Truly. If you're certain.'

Fannie finds herself fixated on the fire iron, burnt black and propped up in the pyramid of wall visible under the virgin's bent knee. Its handle is the head of an animal, or perhaps a mythical creature. Its neck is arched like a proud stallion's, and yet it has a short, pointed beard, as that of a goat. And horns, too. Horns that curl up and out and around on themselves like a lusty satyr's. Fannie squints at it. She needs to distinguish whether it is man or beast. She needs to know if there is anything contained in this strange decorated cavern which might protect her, should she need it. She wonders if it would be too outlandish to ask Mother whether, perhaps, a spell

70

might be cast here, to guard the door against intruders, to ensure their safety, to...

'Fannie,' one of the women says. 'Fannie? If you're certain...'

And eventually Fannie answers. 'Yes.'

Nightfall

By dusk Fannie has learnt that the cavern under the archway is used largely as a resting place – somewhere the girls can wash or warm up or eat an apple or a hunk of bread between customers. Girls flit in and out all day, flapping their shawls like wings, pulling feathers from their own hair and pinning them, quivering, into each other's curls or chignons, swapping skirts and stockings and shoes. Fannie sits hunched beside the fire, waiting for her bones to thaw, and watching. It is a dance and she must study the routine. The lover, the virgin, the rebel – all disappear for two or three hours, return for twenty minutes of embraces and chatter, then slink away through the tunnels again. Their visits are punctuated by those of other girls – perhaps eight or ten of them – who fill the room with colour and laughter. They are not the sorry, moping characters Fannie had imagined they would be in private. They are making the best of their circumstances, whether new or many years entrenched. Fannie understands now why the sailors rush to the bulwarks to peer down at the company they might purchase: it is bright and spirited and intriguing. And by the time the men get close enough to notice that their lace is grimy, that their underthings are moist and soiled, that their pluming perfume cannot disperse the deeper cling of sweat and other men's ejaculate, the pull inside their trousers is too strong to ignore.

They are mirages, these women. And Fannie does not doubt that she, too, can become a convincing mirage. In her experience, that is what being a woman has always meant.

'I wish to start tonight,' Fannie tells Mother, the moment the older woman sails back into the room.

Mother tilts her head. A small trough appears between her pencilled eyebrows. 'It needn't be tonight.'

'I wish it to be.'

'Nobody wishes it to be, child.'

'Very well. Then I need it to be. I haven't much time.'

In response, Mother closes her eyes for a beat too long, as if in mourning for something.

'If you're certain, child, go along with the virgin. You'll make an innocent enough looking pair, with those big eyes.' With the flattened back of her hand, she pushes Fannie's head to left and right. 'Yes. A couple of lost convent girls. That will get them going.'

Fannie endeavours not to focus on the image. She wants only to begin, to push through the pain she knows will come, with the first of them, and convince herself that she can manage it, that it will get better. If this is all she has left to offer her daughter, then so be it.

She shuts her eyes tight to a prayer. It has been so long since last she prayed that she can hardly think how to go about it, and yet, tonight she feels she must. She locks her hands together. *Dear Lord*, she begins…

And that is as far as she gets. What does He, another man, have to offer her?

Within the hour, she is stepping out through the tunnels, a sweet green pear in her shrunken stomach and the virgin prattling at her side. 'The ship that's coming in first, she's been at sea for months, so there'll be a fair stink coming off them, but they'll be quick, so…'

Fannie has trouble concentrating on what is being said, but she does appreciate the distraction of the virgin's sing-song voice. She could not bear to listen to the lonely echo of her heels over the cold ground now. She is scared. And fear is rarely alleviated by silence.

They emerge through the archway under a sagging sky. Shrouds of charcoal cloud have dropped over the ships' masts, reducing the world to a height of fifty feet. Fannie resists the urge to duck under it. She knows she must stand tall if she is going to compete with the others and make enough money to pay for her daughter's medicine.

They hear the ship before they see it: the whining of the wood; the creaking of the ropes; the bawled exchanges between the sailors. What it would be, she thinks again, to sail the oceans on such a vessel, to leave the land at your back and be carried into the sky.

'Don't expect the best pick tonight,' the virgin whispers, leaning close as they swarm along the jetty with a handful of other girls: some Mother's, some not. 'But you'll be pretty again once your hair regrows and then I'd say you'll have your choice. You look a real sweetheart, Fannie.'

I was a sweetheart, once, she thinks.

She is astonished that even here, even now, when she has fallen so low, she is expected to maintain a satisfying appearance. The shock hushes her. She is not a piece of fruit, to be polished and picked and turned about and pinched before purchase. She is only a repository for the unwanted consequence of a transaction. She might just as well be a crumpled kerchief. For a man who has been months at sea, she thinks, she will prove adequate, especially when she is pushed against a wall and her skirts are thrown up over her head and she becomes indistinguishable from the next girl. She is expecting indifference: rough hands and sickening pants; searing pain followed by a raw and lingering soreness – a foul augmentation of how it had felt the very first time.

What she does not account for is how quickly it happens.

She, the virgin, and the other girls reach the end of the jetty in a fog of sugary fragrance and their own sour breaths. The water gurgles and slaps, blackly invisible beneath the moonless sky. Soon, the ship skims into view, sails cracking, hull gently tilting. And inside seconds, it seems, the sailors are clambering onshore, their legs braced wide as cowboys', their upper bodies toppling as they search their balance, the stink of seaweed and desperation throbbing from them.

Fannie clamps her mouth shut and waits, and the sailors come like sharks on a feeding frenzy, grasping girls by the wrists and dragging them away to the music of their companions' hoots and jeers. The jetty grows gradually less crowded, until only Fannie and one other girl remain. Fannie risks a sideways glance at the girl, who is as thin as sticks and twice as knurled. She stands hunched around her scooped out belly, all bulging elbow bones and jutting shoulders. She has her hair at least, Fannie thinks, resisting the urge to put her hand to her shorn scalp. But what does that matter, really? Fannie will never look at herself again. She could not bear to. She has become a creature of the seedy night. She stares at the skinny girl until the girl turns to meet her eye. She nods, tweaks her lips into something like a smile. The skinny girl mirrors her. And then, just as they are beginning to urge bravery to each other, Fannie feels a hand close around her forearm and she is yanked away.

She does not look at the man who has claimed her. She banishes him to the periphery of her sight and leaves him there: less than human; a shade. But he has the unmistakeable strength of a real man as he hauls her through the docks, past the bundled couplings of his friends and their choices in doorways and shadows, and towards a shack which is home to a few battered coracles and hung webs of frayed green fishing net. They haven't any means of getting inside, so he steers Fannie around and behind the shack, where there is no light but the off-white gleam of a string of saliva across his bottom lip. Fannie cannot help but see this as he leans in towards her and, ruffling the cotton of her skirts in his calloused hands, lifts them up around her waist. The sudden rush of cold air makes her want to clench her legs together, but already she knows better than to anger her customer with such a reflex. She stands firm. She looks over his shoulder as he thrusts her skirts into her hands, freeing his own to move to his grubby breeches, which he fumbles with and cannot loose. She begins to count the rich butterscotch orbs of the gas lamps on the nearest streets, the curls of rising chimney smoke, the rhythmic barks of a faraway dog, the number of doors slammed in anger or haste or fear. With a huff, her customer finally liberates himself. He presses closer, flattening one hand against the planked wall above her head. He is hot, somehow, in the bitter night. He smells like the damp, matted earth on the underside of lifted moss. She feels him gape his mouth, as though he is about to speak, and shut it again. Then, with a blunt and careless stab, he ruptures the last flimsy skin of the woman she used to be, and Fannie – that proud, wilful, smiling soul – is shed and sloughs to the ground to settle amongst the fish guts.

Men

She remembers that she will be expected to receive more than one man that night as she stumbles back along the piers, alone, her boots slipping on the newly frosted wood. When he was finished, her first customer had only grunted, shoved the money at her, then turned and walked away – in the direction of a boarding house, she assumes, and a warm bed. She wonders momentarily whether he had been satisfied with his purchase, but before she is able to properly form an opinion on the matter, she lifts a trembling hand and strikes herself, hard, across the cheek. The slap echoes over the rippling water.

She does not care whether he was satisfied or not. She will not care. His enjoyment, or lack thereof, does not detract from the fact that she has earned the money – fairly, if not respectably – and that she can send it to the innkeeper as soon as the sun rises.

As she approaches the archway, her mind on the fire, and that tattered chaise longue, and sleep – it has been such a long while since she slept – she sees the skinny girl being handed from one man to another, like a rag doll a spoilt child has grown tired of. The skinny girl does not resist. She only turns her head away from their smirks and waits. The first man wanders away and the second man pulls at her camisole, tearing the material to expose her tiny breasts to the chill air. Noticing their diminutive size, he grips one, squeezes it hard, painfully, then laughs. The girl does not react to this abuse except to tighten her jaw, and Fannie wants to run to her, and throw that beast aside, and draw the girl to her chest, and hold her so that she might cry and cry, and, when she has recovered herself, ask her what her name is. A name is important. It might just be the only possession that girl has left. Fannie wishes that she could look into her small, grey eyes and listen as she uttered it.

But she will cost the girl her earnings if she interferes, and she would not dare rob her of a prize so unhappily gained.

Look away, she thinks. Keep apart. But whichever direction she turns her head, she is confronted by the strange and frantic tango of men obtaining or discarding women. Skirts balloon and shawls flap and hair soars around in wide, fanned arcs as they dance in the great sordid ballroom below the city. The men all look the same: grubby collars, worn knees, salt-stiffened hair, open mouths.

Fannie walks past the beckoning silence of the archway towards them, because next week, her daughter will require another bottle of medicine, and Fannie is not sure how long she will survive in this rough new world she has dropped into. She must earn what she can tonight, and the night after, and the night after that, and keep folding the money away into envelopes and posting them to her glorious, faraway daughter, until she can suffer it no more: the indignity, the pain, the sadness.

Oh, already she feels the sadness. It is rendering her limbs weighty and cumbersome. It is twisting the muscles of her stomach so that she cannot stand straight-backed. It is shunting bile up her throat. She moves like an automaton, trying to resurrect the joy that once powered her to drift so gracefully around the beautiful parts of this city. She was a ballerina, then. A swan. White wings; an elegant neck; soft feathers; pointed toes. She spun under her gentleman's hooked arm and they laughed. They chased between the cranking and the sparks of the shipbuilders, and shushed each other when they were driven away by shouts and wagged caps. They gripped hands and vanished behind her rippling portière for nights and days, and bucked and moaned and forgot the taste of everything but the other's sticky skin. And though she knows that, were it not for those seemingly perfect hours, she would not have found herself here, they are where her mind goes when the next man takes her between the stilts of the jetty, and the third clamps one hand over her mouth and the other around the base of her skull and forces her against the algae-greened hull of a grounded ship.

The second sailor had been young, timid, polite even. He paused to brush a flop of blond hair off his forehead. He blushed when he dug into his loosened breeches for the money, and both breeches and belt clunked to the sandy ground. And God, was he easier to ignore than this mounting pressure on the back of her neck, and the rising heave caused by feeling her cheek slick against the mouldy algae and the splintered wood beneath, and having her upper body forced so far downwards that she might touch her nose to her knees, and the deep ache brought about by the desperate ram, ram, ramming of the brute at her back.

She holds her breath and tries not to listen to the guttural grunting. She screws her eyes tightly shut and thinks of the river which had poppled past the inn where she left her daughter: she imagines small hands, reaching into clear water to collect pebbles in spectrum shades of brown and grey, violet and jade; a damselfly landing on the crest of her head and flicking its glittering wings before being shaken off by a giggle. She hears the clucks of the chickens as they scutter around the dusty yard. She recalls the trees that stood guard over that trickle of water, their trunks straight as seriousness, and sees her daughter skipping amongst them, following the flitting path of a bird. But her darling girl soon goes too far, and the trees are growing closer together, and she stumbles into darkness, the bird and her senses lost. It is too dangerous, Fannie thinks, without her mother there to watch, to call after her.

The grunting gathers pace.

'Come on, whore,' the third sailor gasps. 'Put a bit of life into it, or I won't be paying you.'

With a strength Fannie thought she had already exhausted, she brings her head and shoulders up against his grasp. She inches her head around to spit at him.

'Then don't pay me. I shan't put an ounce more life into it.'
Ounth.

In an instant, he slips his hand around her neck and forces her head up, as one might a dog with some revolting item held between its teeth.

'Oh, I'm sure you can be persuaded.'

He closes his hand around her windpipe and squeezes. Fannie feels a shifting within.

'No, sir,' she manages to insist. *Thir*. 'You are wrong. You have nothing left to threaten me with. I am already dead.'

And she thinks that perhaps she might be. This is not the body she has inhabited in the past. This one, she has no control over. She cannot fold her slender fingers neatly into her lap. She cannot cross one ankle daintily across the other. She cannot drop her shoulders and lift her chin to ensure that her neck can be admired to the greatest advantage. She is a ghost of that girl. Where then, she wonders, can her true body have gone? Wherever it is, no one will bury her. There is no one. Life has shown her that she is not worth anyone's thoughts or time. She must never have been worth anything at all, to have to endure this, and to have to do so without protest, and to have to be without the daughter she has loved to agony since the moment she emerged, tight-curled and grey and soft-eyed, into the world.

Perhaps her daughter, though... Perhaps her earnest, clever daughter, with her thoughtful ways and her precise hands... Perhaps she will escape this city and its dirty gutters and its crowded shadows. That is Fannie's last hope. That her daughter will fare better. That her daughter will go out into the light, where she will be seen and appreciated and loved.

Long minutes later, when the grunting man has finished, he grabs the back of Fannie's dress in his balled fist, wipes himself dry with it, and then hurls her aside. She lands with a thud against the slippery hull of that abandoned ship, drops onto her backside, and watches him walk away, wide-legged and over-muscled and bull-like. Her insides throb against the phantom of his phallus and she begins to time her breathing to the throb, before she catches and reprimands herself. Think of something other. Keep apart.

She listens for the plashing in and out of the sea, and the stuttered pants of the nearest sailors, and the deceitful moans of the more experienced girls, and the swooping pulse of the wind through pale sails, and she knows that she will not take another tonight. She cannot bear it. She will return to Mother, and she will sleep, and tomorrow... Tomorrow...

Against the stone of the wall to her diagonal left, she detects a movement and every inch of her pulls inward. No more. She shuts like a clamshell around a pearl. Bringing her legs up against her chest, she wraps her arms around her knees, and lowers her head, trying to silence even her thoughts. No more. No more. Despite herself, she chants the words. She is designing an incantation. She is becoming the witch the foreman named her once.

But just as she goes about beginning this transformation, she realises that it is the cat she can see. The plush blue-grey cat, with her coat the colour of dawn or dusk, and her apple-pip eyes, and her languorous stroll.

'You've come to keep me company,' Fannie murmurs, as the cat slinks nearer and pushes her head against Fannie's legs. Fannie reaches out a hand, to run it along her back as she did before, to trace her tiny bones and know the tender touch of another being, but she cannot reach. The cat's back bows as she tiptoes further from Fannie's fingertips. The hairs on Fannie's arms stand, as though they too are stretching out for the animal, but the cat only mewls and pads away, and soon she is nothing more than a rumour in the mist.

'Wait. Please,' Fannie whispers. 'Please come back.'

But though she squints into the churning mists for the longest while, the cat does not return, and Fannie drops her head back onto her knees and closes her eyes and finally slips into the empty dark.

Life

'Wake up.' It is a woman's voice, pitched low and roughened by too much cigarette smoke. Fannie keeps her eyes closed, despite the persistent jostling at her shoulder. She does not want to wake up. She wants to sleep and sleep, so that she can dream of her daughter's frown as she struggled to decipher the meaning of the hands of a clock, or her daughter's nose, wrinkled in disgust at the bitter tang of an orange.

'Fannie!' the voice says again, louder this time.

Fannie shifts, grumbles. 'Who's asking?'

'Christ, Fannie. You're so pale I thought for a minute you were dead.'

'I'm alive,' Fannie replies, peeling her lids open just far enough to see that morning has swooped over the docks, bright and blue as a kingfisher. The galleons' neglected white sails swell proudly. 'Though I did have my doubts yesterday.'

A rounded laugh. 'Would you listen to that?' the voice says. 'She's still got a sense of humour, so she'll muscle through, I'll wager. Get up, won't you. Good Lord, you're frosted over.' A hand begins brushing at Fannie's shoulder, making a rasping sound when the warm skin meets the iced fabric. 'You can't have sat there all night.'

Fannie nods. 'I was watching out for the cat,' she says.

'What bleeding cat?'

Fannie coaxes her eyes to focus on the darkened shape leaning over her. It is large, huffing, warm. It's the sort of body you might hurl yourself at and be enveloped by. Mother, of course.

'The cat...'

She closes her eyes in search of the words and, when she opens them again, a sleek curtain of hair falls into her sights, shone to gleaming ruby by the low sun, and she realises that it is not Mother who has come in search of her. *We'll look after you, Fannie*, the rebel had said, and it seems she had meant it.

'It was ... just a cat. It doesn't matter.'

But Fannie is convinced that it does, somehow – that the cat showed her the way to the letter-writer's house and that it will show her the way again. The words come unbidden into her mind – *a familiar* – but she does not want to share them with the rebel, does not want to indulge in that oldest of men's fictions.

'Right,' the rebel continues, wrapping an arm around Fannie's ribcage and hoisting her up. 'Well, come on. Let's get you some breakfast.'

Fannie lets herself be ushered through the docks like an invalid. She leans on the rebel and takes small, shuffling steps, on account of the pain between her legs, yes, but also because she wants to appreciate the morning – the relief of its coming.

The shouts of sailors and the thuds of stacked crates echo in the still air. Great barrels of dead fish are being unloaded: she can smell their briny stink, hear the sloshing of the chilled water. Above, gulls spin and spin, following the back and forth of the men as they stride up and down the plank to collect another barrel, haul it onto the jetty, return for the next. Their cries are the wails of ghosts. The ships do not move today, but their sails continue to breathe. They *aah* on the in-breath, *umph* on the out. *Aah-umph. Aah-umph.* It is the most glorious heartbeat sound. Fannie remembers putting her daughter to sleep on her own pillow, so that she could lie alongside her, press an ear to her peach-round middle, and listen to her heart growing stronger and stronger. Fannie does not ask the rebel where they are going. She does not want to be told that they will soon scurry back underground with the rats. The morning is rowdy and colourful, and she wants to see it all before she is plunged back into darkness. She wants to run along the jetty and join in hauling the barrels. She wants to become a sailor. She wants to be able to take on the world as a man might, with a map and a fair wind.

When they pass the archway, Fannie looks a question at the rebel: *In there?*

The rebel's angular face softens.

'Oh, no. Only between jobs,' she says. 'We're going to Mother's now.'

Not in the slums, Fannie thinks. Not back to the slums. But she does not want the rebel to hear her say *thlumth* and pity her still-swollen mouth, so she only follows, contemplating the dark beauty of the shadows which criss-cross – *crith-croth* – the docks and stretch up into the city.

'There'll be a bed for you there,' the rebel explains. 'Not for you alone, mind. Sharing. But comfortable for all that. And we've some creams you can use, you know, for the chafing. Some secret ingredients Mother won't let us in on, but she keeps plenty put by. I think its whale fat and oil of wintergreens, personally, but whatever it is, it's soothing afterwards.'

'Thank you,' Fannie says. 'But do you think...? I need to get to the letter-writer's house.'

'It can't wait?'

Fannie shakes her head.

'I'll go with you,' the rebel answers. Then, sternly, 'But breakfast first.'

They climb up out of the docklands and begin walking the route Fannie always took to the factory, away from the slums, along the promenade. At the place where Fannie would have turned amongst the merchant's buildings, they continue along the front, where the waves venture in further to kiss the sea wall.

Fannie parts her lips a little to let the rising sea spray onto her tongue. It tastes like fear and freedom, and she imagines herself suspended on her back, her arms outstretched, swilling about in the shallows. She imagines the cold and the cradling of the tides. It would be welcome, she thinks, even if she never washed back ashore.

The sun is warming the city to steam by the time they reach

Mother's, and feeling a thawing in her back and shoulders, Fannie finally releases the rebel's arm.

The dwelling is a dilapidated three-storey townhouse, which leans into its neighbour as though drunk. Tangled green stems writhe through the slipped roof tiles. The chimney has crumbled and tilts in the opposite direction to the rest of the building, giving the impression that nothing is straight: not the painted window frames, which are flaking from deep green to silver birch; not the stonework, which is mossed in patches; not the jointed gutter pipes. The ground floor is a tavern, shut up until dusk, the rebel explains, after which its doors are flung open to allow sailors and merchants and gamblers in, and cigar smoke, scandal, and brawls out. The first and second floors, though, are reserved for Mother's girls.

As they go inside and ascend the stairs, their boots clomping over the bare wood, the rebel explains the rules.

'You can stay sometimes or all the time, if you've nowhere else to be. Mother doesn't ask any questions. The rent is reasonable – a percentage of what you earn each night, not a set amount, so you don't need to wear yourself to the bone. Mother comes and goes, but she doesn't sleep here. Some of the girls say she doesn't sleep at all, that she stays always awake, to watch over some poor girl or other. That's nonsense, if you ask me. But you won't find a better madam in this city, I can promise you that. Her only insistence is that you don't work the pub downstairs. Business on the streets, not in your beds – that's what she says.' The rebel pauses, turns from her waist only to look back down the stairs and, finding Fannie's eye, shrugs. 'And I think that's more than fair, don't you?'

Fannie nods, which elicits a smile from the rebel.

They reach the top of the stairs and the rebel steers Fannie through a door which is already ajar. She closes it behind them with a thunk and they are cloaked by the warmth in the room. The curtains – dusty but a thick burgundy velvet – are not drawn and sunlight falls through the salt-blasted panes in cloudy planks. Beneath a large, ornate mantle, a fire crackles and dances. Near the windows, there are three cushioned settees which, though evidently well-worn and creased, look so welcoming that Fannie fears she might collapse into one and never stand again. On the far side of the room, against a wall on which a bumpy oil-painted seascape has been hung over wilted wallpaper, there is an old dining table, laid with baskets of bread and eggs and a jug of milk.

'Help yourself, child,' says a deep voice at Fannie's back.

She swings around to find that in place of the rebel stands Mother, panting from her climb up the stairs. Fannie flinches, surprised by the sudden switch, but does not allow a question over her tongue. She will not say anything which might tilt her out of this precarious position.

'There isn't much,' Mother continues. 'Only this one meal for the day. Anything more you'll have to find for yourself. But there's always enough to share.'

Fannie braces herself and makes sure to step slowly across the threadbare rug towards the table. She will not rush. She will not glut.

When she hovers a hand over the baskets, deciding where to begin, she realises that she is trembling. Not from the cold, which might be forgotten in this warm room, but, she supposes, from the shock. Last night was a shock. A physical fright. Though her mind has resigned itself to what she must do, her body is fighting it. Discovering she was with child after her gentleman disappeared was frightening, too, but it was a happy fright; her body had bloomed with it and she had known that it was right.

She rolls an egg into her palm and cups it, testing how firmly she will have to squeeze before the frail shell cracks. It takes only the slightest pressure to fracture the chill surface. Fannie considers the dark line which jags down its pale brown curve, then pushes a fingernail into it, peels the plump white egg free, and holds it up in front of her face. It seems to her a vulnerable thing. She cannot remember the last time she ate a boiled egg. Opening her mouth, she puts it between her remaining teeth and bites down into the springy flesh. The yoke crumbles onto her tongue and she swallows a swell of nausea. It is too rich, too full. She grips the table.

'Sit down,' Mother urges. 'Eat. Give yourself time.'

Fannie shakes her head. 'I don't have time. The letter-writer.'

'The letter-writer,' Mother sighs. 'Yes. But only after some bread. Then I'll find a girl to go with you.'

And even as she says it, she is loosening, changing. Her sprung hair smooths itself flat, and her shoulders narrow, and her petticoats shrink, and, in a strange, pulsing moment, she is the rebel again.

Fannie grips the table tighter with one hand and brings the other to her stomach. She thinks perhaps she will eject the boiled egg after all. Or else that she might faint. She feels herself on the verge – that her mind will follow close behind her body, for she cannot have seen what she believes she has just seen.

One woman cannot become another so easily.

And yet, here she stands ... Fannie ... the evidence of the fact that one might. Perhaps the truth is that no woman is ever really known. A woman is only assumed about, and then denied the chance to speak against the assumption. A woman is told how and what and when. And so she pushes her truest self far down, where she can close her eyes and ears to the speculations. A woman carries secrets as deep as her petticoats, because she must. And if she is not known, then perhaps she might become anything at all, perhaps she might transform, perhaps...

Fannie wonders slowly whether she might have been drugged. Whether the food is laced with laudanum. Happen this has all been Mother's trick – to bind Fannie to the docks and the dirty deals made there. It might be that she traps her girls this way, that she drugs them to keep them working. Fannie sways where she stands. She does not know anything anymore, except that everything is changing. She looks to the seascape on the wall, and feels the waves roll beneath her feet.

'You're too weak to be alone this morning,' the rebel says. And her voice is higher than Mother's, but if both women could leap the span of twenty years, they might be one and the same. Fannie's head whirls at the thought. The rebel become the mother. The mother hatched from the rebel.

'I'll get stronger,' she insists. 'I have always been strong enough. I must be, for my daughter.'

'The child,' says the rebel.

Fannie nods slowly. 'She's unwell. She needs medicine. I have to send the money before the week's end. Every week, more money.'

Fannie rips a small hunk of bread from the loaf and pushes it to the back of her mouth, where it will not touch her tender gums, then chews and chews. It is enough. Her stomach no longer growls. She eyes the door, feels in her pocket for the pittance the three sailors paid her. Together with that she already had saved from the factory, it will cover the week, just. She will need to earn more tonight if she is to pay Mother's rent, make up for the lost time.

She attempts some quick calculations. Would four men each night of the week be enough? Twenty-eight men in seven shifts. Can she even attract twenty-eight customers without her hair and her teeth? She supposes she can, so long as the other girls stay busy. She is beginning to understand now why they crowd to the end of the jetty together. They need each other. They have become a singular creature. The men have made it so.

'You must be tired, too,' she says. 'You don't need to come with me.'

The rebel waves Fannie's concerns away with a flick of the wrist she has surely learnt or inherited from Mother. Fannie wonders how long the rebel has been embroiled in this game. Months? Years? The thought saddens her too much and she shoves it away.

'I'm coming with you,' the rebel answers. 'We'll be quicker together. We'll send the money, then we'll come back and we'll sleep.'

Oh, Fannie needs that. At the word 'sleep', a softening sensation runs through her body, from head to toe tip. She envisages herself reclining on a deep mattress with such intensity that she feels her body tipping into it. Perhaps this is the beginning of the collapse, she thinks, but she does not release the table. She does not let go. And somehow, despite the ache at her core, and the pounding behind her eyes, and the thin tearing between her legs, she finds herself stepping back down the stairs, through the door, and out into the morning.

Dawn

'I know a short cut,' the rebel says, and Fannie follows wordlessly, secretly relieved to have even these small decisions – of when and where to turn – made for her. She has little capacity left for thinking. Battling her exhaustion is utilising every fold of her mind. The rebel leads Fannie along residential streets she does not know, and past factories she does, between rows of shops she could never afford to visit, and through the park where Fannie and her gentleman plunged into the lake that silly, moonlit night.

It was colder than the grave, that lake, and Fannie could go in no further than her waist. Water purled around her sodden skirts and nipped at the skin of her thighs and stomach, even through the layered fabric, which darkened in wild, wet blooms. Her love splashed at her and she splashed back, but where he stood tall and unaffected by the temperatures, Fannie soon found her shoulders, her chest, her arms curling around her middle, where a deep, pervasive chill had begun to spread. It was as though all those throbbing organs hidden within her had been dragged free and tossed onto a slab of ice. Fannie felt herself violated by that cold. Eviscerated. Later, when she realised she was with child, she considered that perhaps she had already felt a stirring inside her; that she was, subconsciously, desperate to protect some small, perfect life.

And so it has been, she thinks. Ever since. So it always will be.

The memory of her gentleman, his shirt tails floating on the surface of the lake, is strong enough to persuade her heart to beat a fraction quicker, and she wishes she could expunge it. She knows it is impossible. Six years gone and she still blushes at the way his trousers had clung around his crotch. She'd blushed then, though she'd known he wouldn't give a dash who looked or saw. He taught her something of liberation during those happy months. But not enough to stand as tall and loose as he did, his arms hanging without purpose at his sides, his beautiful head cocked at a playful diagonal, his legs set wide in readiness for his next bout of tomfoolery. The short, fair curls which usually bounced away from his forehead dripped down over his eyebrows, and he lifted a hand to push them back; an arc of water droplets followed, catching the silvery light, and Fannie laughed at how handsome he was, that man of hers. At how easy he was. At how definitely he knew himself, and, in turn, how willing the world was to recognise it.

'Do you never tire of gazing at me?' her love had teased.

Fannie is sorry now that she hadn't spent more time looking inward. This all might have played out differently, if only she had been granted the freedom to know herself as well as did that man.

They reach the letter-writer's house with the rattle of a passing milk cart. The empty bottles jostle and chink and Fannie watches them for a moment, fighting for their place in this clamouring city, before she turns and raps on the painted black door. The letter-writer answers on the instant and beckons her inside.

'Your friend, too,' he says, flicking his eyes at the rebel, who is fidgeting on the front step.

The rebel bows her head and crosses the threshold with such piety that she might just as well be entering a church. Fannie stifles a smile. She is beginning to feel lighter, now that she is here, and the letter-writer is positioning his pen over a blank new page, and the money has weight inside her pocket, and she can believe that soon it will be travelling towards her daughter. Her clever, tippy-toed daughter. Her smiling sunflower girl. Her wild, dainty, furious beauty. Fannie breathes for her.

With a nod, the letter-writer loops and links her words across the page – about how she can meet the additional cost of the medicine, about how she has secured a position which will allow her to continue to do so, about the new address to which the innkeeper might send her correspondence. If the letter-writer knows the address, he does not betray any opinion on it as he sets it down on the paper.

'Anything else, miss?' He cocks his head, his freckled hand still poised to drop into another string of words. He considers Fannie over the half-rim of his glasses.

Fannie parts her lips to say *no*. There is nothing more she can promise. Unless...

A flutter starts up at her middle, as faintly hopeful as a hummingbird's beating heart. She could, after she's earned enough... She might...

'May I include a note for my daughter?' she asks, breathless at the assembling idea. She trusts the innkeeper or his wife will read it to her. Haven't they always been kind to her daughter? Haven't they nursed her through each worsening bout of ill health? When first she had news, Fannie could hardly believe her joyful girl had succumbed to sickness so quickly, but her worry had soon drowned out any doubt.

'Of course.' The letter-writer plucks up a clean sheet of paper and flourishes it over the first. 'What should it say?'

'It should say...' Fannie inhales deeply. 'It should say, *I will come to find you soon, my love. Each night, before you fall asleep, say a prayer for your mother, and one morning, not too very long from now, you will wake to find me there beside you.*'

She taps her right foot against the boarded floor as she listens to the even scratch of the pen. She fidgets with the cuff of her sleeve. These words she cannot bear to look at, for fear that her daughter will have forgotten the shape of her face and will not recognise her; for fear that she has spoken too soon and the time will be too long; for fear that she will not manage to make them come true. But then, she thinks, to love is to embrace fear, isn't it? And she can do nothing but love, love, love her glowing girl.

'The young lady's name?' the letter-writer asks.

Fannie can hardly speak it, so precious are its sounds. She runs her tongue across her lips, to unglue them. A little crack sounds as she opens her jaw and she closes her eyes against the third of her customers, who had held her mouth wide, who had pushed in and in. She cannot send her daughter's name over a tongue still tainted by him. She will not.

'Address it, please, to My Little Swan,' she says.

'Very well.'

She leans closer as he spills the letters over the page: a large, curlicued L; a closely looped e; a symmetrically twisted S... It is as pretty as Fannie had hoped it would be.

He hands Fannie the envelope.

'I don't know how to thank you,' she says. She will not offer this stained and kindly man the money he has already refused. She will not insult him so.

'I do,' says the rebel, and swooping down, she kisses him firmly on the cheek then shrieks with laughter when his eyes bulge above his glasses. 'Now hurry, Fannie. We'll catch first post if we're swift.'

Fannie tarries. It feels ungrateful, to run out on the letter-writer so abruptly. Fannie glances at him; he nods his approval.

Seeing this, the rebel grabs her wrist and barrels them both back through the door, and before Fannie can protest, they are running down the middle of the road, dodging snorting horses and curses, tripping over their skirts, clutching their bonnets to their heads, stumbling into passers-by and bumping wheeled perambulators, and all the while Fannie clutches the letter so tight she fears her knuckle bones might burst through her skin. She has it all, finally: the note; the money; the promise. And soon it will be with her daughter and she will be able to breathe again. She grins stupidly as they caper along, ignoring the constriction at her chest, the throbbing of her gums, the tearing between her legs.

'Look at this morning,' the rebel gasps, spinning around to indicate the dramatic flame-and-bloom sky with the sweep of a slender arm.

They slow into a skipping sort of walk, tipping their heads back, because it is magnificent. And eerie. Fannie had hardly noticed it during the walk to Mother's boarding house. Or rather, she thinks, it has changed since. It is shifting even now. Second on second, the sky is darkening. It is too fast for the simple descent of dusk, even if it were the right time. Suddenly and yet too slowly, the factory workers, the head-hung horses, the prostitutes, the frisking dogs, the departing birds, the newspaper boys, the street hawkers, the scuttling rats, the bartering merchants, the huddled lovers, the wind itself – all, in turn, fall silent as an enormous blood moon glides before the soft morning sun and blots out its flaring light. Soon, only a thin, gleaming halo remains. Within it sits a vast black disc: a hole, descending towards the end of everything; or a tunnel, leading somewhere new.

Fannie turns to observe a storytelling of crows scrawking apart towards the angled grey heights of the city's chimney tops. Beyond, another horde panics amongst the highest branches.

'They're going to roost,' Fannie whispers. Ready voices are

not welcome under this strange, tainted sky. 'Why should they be going to roost now? What could they need to escape?'

'There is always something terrible,' the rebel replies.

Fannie shakes her head but does not turn to meet her new friend's eye. 'No,' she says. 'Not always.'

But she cannot deny that the entire world is fading and flattening. That the ships in the docks have stilled. That the wheels of the nearby carriages have ceased grinding over the cobbles. That even the leaves of the maple trees along the main boulevard have stopped stirring. It is as though all is growing less colourful, less deep, less real.

Fannie feels light-headed yet heavy-bodied. There is a vague sense that nothing that has happened in the past two days has happened to her. She cannot recall how it feels, to truly be in possession of her own sense of self. Inside her boots, she spreads her toes then relaxes them again. Next, she bends her knees slightly. Then she tenses the muscles in her thighs. Slowly, methodically, she works her way up her entire body: feeling, tightening, loosing, holding. She reminds herself of every part of herself – her elegant fingers, the graceful length of her neck – and finally she focuses on her mind. Inside her balded skull is contained the portrait of every moment she has spent with her daughter. Every cotton-folded bedtime. Every tangle-haired walk along the promenade. Every red-cheeked temper tantrum. Every steaming tin bath-time. Every tear shed in confusion at their tiny, insular life. Every dancing morning, when she knelt on the mattress and bounced and bounced into the new day. And that is all Fannie needs. The men –

however many there must be – will not cow her. The life will not shatter her. Even the dropping sky will not intimidate her, because one day – whether sooner or later – she will return to the inn to collect her daughter, and they will walk away hand in hand, and they will begin again together, that knotted pair, and they will be in need of nothing but each other.

Fannie wants to weep at the idea, but she won't. Not here. She swallows the tightness gathering in her throat and brings up a sudden cough in its place. She leans forwards and cups her hand over her mouth as her ribcage spasms painfully. When she straightens up and removes her hand, she finds her palm splattered with bright red beads.

'What is that?' the rebel asks, taking hold of Fannie's wrist and tilting her hand outwards for inspection. 'That's blood, Fannie. Are you unwell?'

Fannie shakes her head. 'It's nothing. I just... Before this morning, I hadn't eaten for some time.'

'You're certain?'

Fannie wants to admit to the rebel that she is not. That she had begun the week believing she would still be walking daily to and from the garment factory, scurrying past the docks, pricking her fingers on needle points for twelve straight hours and sucking the blood away, steeling her stomach against the glare of the foreman; that two sweeps of the moon have changed her life in unimaginable ways, and that she fears she will never know certainty again. But she does not want to give up the idea that has flitted across her mind, of she and her daughter, and a sun-shone country lane...

'Let's run a little more,' she says. It seems the only way to calm the churning at her middle. She needs to pound her feet over the streets. She needs to rush along and feel the breeze against her face. She needs to keep going until her breath fails her and she is forced to stop, heaving, and hang over her knees to recover.

'Aren't you tired?' the rebel replies.

'Yes. But I'm not ready to stop yet.'

They take off again, wheeling from street to street, and Fannie's skin is cold and her body is warm, and soon they are laughing at the frivolity of it. With every footfall, the sun is revealed again by another degree, and Fannie feels it is because of her – that she is towing that fearsome moon behind her. Today, she is strong enough. Today, she is as powerful as any witch. Today, she knows magic. The letter in her hand and the money in her pocket is proof of it. She pushes ahead with a new surge of energy as the sun and the city and the sky are finally returned to themselves, and she knows then that she – she alone – can effect change.

As they stream along the boulevard, passing in and out of the dappled shadows of the maple trees, Fannie catches sight of the cat, gambolling along beside them, her tail flowing behind her like a cast feather boa. She is as plush as she was the first time Fannie saw her.

'The cat,' Fannie rasps, and as if in answer, the cat picks up her speed and veers into the street and runs ahead of them, a grey-blue ripple, as fluid as a thought. Fannie charges after her, knowing, somehow, that she will lead her where she needs to go. That she can be trusted. That, whatever it might mean, she is familiar.

She reaches out for the rebel's hand and they clasp fingers tightly, tugging each other through their mismatched strides and laughing all the harder for it. And how good the warmth of another's hand feels to Fannie. How spurring. This, above all else, is what she has needed.

'I had a dream like this once,' she breathes, and she smiles and smiles, because here, in this singular whistling moment, what lies ahead of her, finally, is possibility.

A feeling she had forgotten starts to niggle at her. It is something like a swelling, she supposes – like the surfacing of a breathless seal from a surging roller, or the rising of a hot-air balloon, or the first pitch and rush of love. It is a buoyancy. It is lifting her. Hope, she thinks; it is called hope. And she floats on it, all the way back to the docks, where the sudden sight of Mother standing, arms tight across her chest, face severe as a long gaol sentence, punctures it and sends Fannie plummeting towards the dirty ground. She begins again to cough, but this time, she cannot stop so easily, she cannot catch her breath. Blood clogs her throat – thick and bitter. She hangs over her knees and, with each splutter, stars burst before her eyes and they are blindingly black.

Stolen

When finally Fannie's coughing stops, Mother cocks her mouth and shrugs. 'You're too late,' she says. 'They're all out cold.'

The rebel shifts sideways to peer over Mother's shoulder and down towards the jetties. 'All of them?' she asks.

'Every last one,' Mother replies.

Only then does Fannie notice the stillness: no hollers; no thuds; no bartering. The three women go to lean over the balustrade and consider the sight below. All across the docks, sailors slump over drained barrels or into each other; they sprawl, starfish-like, over the jetties; they snore, tucked up like kittens atop enormous coils of rope. They are harmless, weak.

'They docked with a shipload of rum,' Mother continues, 'and kept a few barrels for their pleasure. The eclipse put them in a strange humour, I'd say. They've already drunk themselves into oblivion.'

'What will we do?' the rebel mouths. They are speaking in whispers, loath to disturb the men they really ought to charm awake.

They listen to the gentle pulse of the waves, pushing into the dock then flowing out, the occasional snap of the galleon's sails. Fannie thinks of that seascape hanging in Mother's lodgings: the thick bumps left behind by the liberal application of oils; the pure white spindrift she had almost been able to feel on her face. She recalls the first time she met Mother, when she had imagined her a wild and fearsome figurehead. She knows then what they must do.

'We could take the ship.'

Mother and the rebel exchange a quizzical look, but they do not laugh at Fannie's suggestion. Though spoken quietly, the confidence in her words is unmistakable. When she hears no protest, she speaks again, louder.

'We should take the ship.' Already there seems to Fannie no other option. She can taste the salt on her lips, feel a cold wind slicing through her clothes. She recognises the rolling fright of knowing there is nothing beneath but water. It would be like flying.

'We can't sail a ship,' the rebel points out.

A grin spreads quick across Mother's face. Her eyes flash. 'What's to stop us learning?'

The rebel releases a panicked laugh. 'You're mad!'

'No,' Fannie replies. 'We're brave.'

Clasping hands, the three women proceed down a set of stone steps – shaded and slime-slippy, even on this bright morning – and duck under the archway into the cavern. The fire has been doused and the air is hung with smoke, but the smoke is nowhere near as thick as the anxiety which clouds the room as the women wonder where they will find enough custom to earn their keep. Where usually the lover and the virgin would be draped over the chaise longue, today they perch on its edge, knees held neatly together, jackets buttoned up to their necks. They are flanked by two more girls Fannie knows only as the mystic and the sage. Another paces the faded rag of rug, swinging her arms before and behind her like a boxer limbering up for a fight – the huntress. Perhaps, Fannie thinks, when they are aboard the ship, the parts they play will be cast aside and she will learn their true names. She trusts it will be so. Having no men onboard to trade their bodies with, what would be the need of such reductive brandings?

'Gather up anything you can,' Mother says, flapping her hands arbitrarily around the sparse room. 'We're to leave anon.'

'To go where?' asks the lover, rising.

'On an adventure,' Mother returns.

Anticipation twists in Fannie's stomach. To step on board a real ship and sail into the morning. To be only amongst these women, who have shown her such kindness. To set off on an adventure all of her own. The anticipation twists again and turns into dread.

'My daughter,' Fannie blurts. 'I need to get her back first. She has to come with us.'

Mother turns to Fannie and Fannie is struck, again, by the older woman's mesmerism. Her small eyes gleam with promise. The confusion of coloured shawls she wears make a mystery of her body. Fannie has no idea who Mother is beneath her rouge and her silks and her jewellery. She is any woman, every woman.

'We'll take her with us, of course. We'll get her back. But not today.'

Fannie nods against her rising tears and Mother grips her upper arm, squeezes, then releases it.

'She belongs with you,' Mother says. 'You'll get her back. But now, you must hold your nerve. You were right – we should take the ship. We've earned it, don't you think?'

'Yes,' is all Fannie can manage to reply.

Soon, the lover and the mystic cradle small bundles in their laps. Fannie cannot imagine what they contain. None of them owns anything beyond her own sense of self. The rebel has pulled on a coat and wound her hair into a scarf. The virgin is biting at her lip. The huntress ceases her pacing and, finally, the girls gather in a clutch at the doorway.

'All right. Quietly about it, then,' Mother says.

They creep out of the cavern, along the tunnel, and out into the brilliant, salt stung morning. No trace remains of that strange, fleet darkening Fannie and the rebel had witnessed as they left the letter-writer's house. The sky is high and creamy blue as it rises away from the last hints of its phoenix-feathered dawn. The air, so close to the water, is chill and clean. The galleon they are to commandeer joggles gently, bumping against the softened wood of the jetty now and then, its sails hardly rippling. A lone gull flaps down to settle on her mast, ruffles its wings, snaps its head to left and right, then hauls itself into flight again and lazes away.

'There she is,' Mother breathes. The women move as one towards the galleon, Mother leading them, as though she really is the figurehead of a grand vessel and they comprise the prow, the hull, the sails.

With the sailors still incapacitated, the docks remain quiet, and the women's heels thunder over the wood as though they number an army. Fannie glances about herself: at the lover's tawny curls; at the virgin's slender shoulders; at the mystic's swinging skirts; at the sage's raised chin. They will make a fine crew – these fearless women, her brave daughter – and they will sail to all the corners of the Earth with only the moon and the tides to guide them. They will become pirates, hunting the treasure of their own lives.

Fannie, buoyed again by the idea, begins to laugh. Mother whips her head around to shush her, but Fannie can do nothing to settle herself. Her voice echoes off the city walls. She clamps her lips shut, but the sound pushes its way out. Already, they are making too much noise. Already, they are forgetting the silence they have been subjected to all this time.

'Hurry, then,' Mother huffs.

Fannie grabs the rebel's wrist and tugs. In response, the rebel barks out a laugh.

'Lord!' says Mother. 'Quickly.'

They begin to scuttle along the jetty. Fannie's hilarity is contagious and soon, the virgin, the lover, the sage, the mystic, even the huntress, are shrieking with excitement. They are urged on by their own voices. They step quicker, Fannie skipping ahead, and soon they are running along the jetty, the planked wood bouncing beneath the pound of their feet, and the virgin's lissom limbs seem to belong to each of them, and they all wear Fannie's wild grin, and they are propelled towards the galleon by Mother's unbreakable confidence, and Fannie can hardly keep track of who is who, so muddled are they, so close are they, so united are they by this rush to freedom.

It is the men, this time, who will be left stranded on the docks.

'Here we come,' Fannie gasps. And she is laughing and weeping, because soon she will be with her daughter again, and she will be able, finally, to offer her what she has wished to offer since the day she took her first tentative breath – the whole world.

Author's Note

Since Victor Hugo's epic novel *Les Misérables* published in 1862, there have been countless adaptations made for stage and screen, and I have been a fan of many. As a child, I played the VHS of the 10th Anniversary Concert until the picture jumped and distorted. I loved every character. Valjean was a hero and a heartthrob. Eponine was brave and entrancing. As I grew older and started to consider my own status as a woman in society, however, it was Fantine's role that most held my fascination. She was, it seemed to me, as brave as Eponine, as goodhearted as Valjean, as firm in her convictions as the dogged Javert. But her storyline was shaped always around the other players. She is abandoned by Félix, cast out by the factory foreman, abused by her customers when she turns to prostitution, arrested by Javert as punishment for her desperation. When, finally, a man does show her kindness, it comes too late: she is close to death. It felt to me as though Fantine existed always in relation to these men, as though she had no agency. But who would she be, I wondered, if the male characters were stripped from the story? What would happen if she attempted to save herself? *Fannie* is my imagining of that scenario. It is Fantine's story and no one else's. Just like the hope she never relinquishes, it belongs to her.

Acknowledgements

When I started work on this short novel, following a trip to the theatre to watch the musical version of *Les Misérables*, I had no readership in mind. I was writing out of frustration and I was enjoying the release it allowed me. It is perhaps true that all of my writing grows from frustration – at an idea, an unfairness, an unanswered question – together with the feeling of joy gained by the act of writing itself: it is my way to set one against the other. But I wasn't sure where *Fannie* belonged. It is obvious now that she belongs with Honno, a press long-committed to women and their experiences of the world, their stories, and their voices. So I must thank everyone at Honno for championing this story, and I must especially thank Janet Thomas, for her keen editorial eye and for her belief in two women: Fannie and me.

I must also, as ever, thank those friends and family who (largely) have little interest in books, but who listen to me talk about them endlessly anyway. Your kindness does not go unnoticed.

And finally, I must thank those of you who have taken the

time to read this story. There is no greater joy for me than sharing my writing with readers, and I appreciate every one of you enormously.

ABOUT HONNO

Honno Welsh Women's Press was set up in 1986 by a group of women who felt strongly that women in Wales needed wider opportunities to see their writing in print and to become involved in the publishing process. Our aim is to develop the writing talents of women in Wales, give them new and exciting opportunities to see their work published and often to give them their first 'break' as a writer. Honno is registered as a community co-operative. Any profit that Honno makes is invested in the publishing programme. Women from Wales and around the world have expressed their support for Honno. Each supporter has a vote at the Annual General Meeting. For more information and to buy our publications, please write to Honno at the address below, or visit our website: www.honno.co.uk

Honno, 14 Creative Units, Aberystwyth Arts Centre
Aberystwyth, Ceredigion SY23 3GL

Honno Friends

We are very grateful for the supportof all our Honno Friends. For more information on how you can become a Honno Friend, see:https://www.honno.co.uk/about/support-honno/